Perfume Princess

KRISTINA MIRANDA

Parapet Publishing Co. October 2013

ISBN: 10: 0615877184
ISBN-13: 978-0615877181

For Gaby, my reluctant princess

One

"Perfume: any smell that is used to drown a worse one."

~Elbert Hubbard

"Welcome…um…home, Miss Lily."

Mom's doorman stumbles over the words as he rests my luggage on the polished marble floor. Even he knows how I feel about being here. How wrong it is to call Mom's two-story Manhattan penthouse, *home*.

I scan the foyer, taking in the heavy scent of perfume, flowers, and furniture polish. Nothing's changed. Welcome to the museum would be more like it. I try to conjure up the smell of fresh baled hay and sunshine, to no avail.

"I'll take them from here, George. Really, you didn't need to come up." I make my voice sound as cheerful as possible. I've had enough sympathy for one day. First from Dad, when he hugged me goodbye in Houston. Then from Mom's driver, Curtis, when he picked me up from the airport alone—without Mom or Jas. And now from George. I give him a little wave and watch the elevator close.

I'm glad none of Mom's personal assistants are anywhere to be seen. They're probably off running ridiculous errands, as usual. I drag my suitcase toward the spiral staircase, checking to make sure it's not leaving any marks on the floor. I wouldn't want Ingrid to be fired on account of me—if she still works for Mom, that is.

Central Park looms below the living room window, comforting me—a little. It's not Texas, but at least it's a place where I can breathe. I pause for a moment to take in the view, then switch arms and give my suitcase another pull. Before I make it to the staircase, I hear someone in the foyer.

"Ingrid? Ingrid!"

Mom already? Her high heels click across the floor. I take a deep breath.

"Lily, darling!" Mom gives me a stiff hug and kisses both my cheeks. "Curtis explained the situation, correct? Last minute details for the perfume launch." She glances down at my scuffed-up cowboy boots and then at the hole in my jeans. "We couldn't make it to the airport this afternoon. How was your flight?"

"It was—"

"Have you seen Ingrid?"

I shake my head.

"Go unpack. And change, for heaven's sake. We have a dinner reservation." Mom makes her way down the hall. "And why didn't George bring those bags up to your room?"

"Where's Jas?" I ask.

Mom doesn't turn around. "She's at Marco's. Getting her nails done for the shoot tomorrow." Mom pulls off her silk scarf and glances back at me. "Too bad you couldn't have gone with her. Those eyebrows are like bird nests."

Her words roll off me, harmless. You can't hurt someone who doesn't care. "I love birds!" I chirp.

I make my way up the staircase, dragging my bags from step to step, and finally make it to my room, a.k.a. the guest room. I drop my luggage just inside the door. I know Mom wants me to change, but what's inside my suitcase is no better than what I've got on. At least according to her.

On the dresser sits a copy of Mom's best-selling book, *Any Woman Can be Beautiful: The French Way to Fabulous.* Is this a hint? She already sent me a copy months ago. I stick it inside the drawer so I don't have to look at it, then plop down on the bed and cover my head with a pillow.

How will I ever make it through the summer? And worse, what will Fire Star do without me? Poor horse. She doesn't like anyone else to ride her. My eyes burn, but I won't cry. What good would that do?

~~~

"Mom's going to freak if you wear that." Jasmine shakes her head and looks through the meager display of clothing I just finished hanging in the closet.

"Is there a dress code or something?" I set a picture of Dad standing next to Fire Star on the dresser. "I thought it was just some sushi place—which you and Mom know I don't eat, by the way."

"We're going to Asuka's. Best sushi in Manhattan. But don't worry; they have other things you can eat, too." She takes a pair of dark jeans off a hanger. "At least these don't have rips in them."

"All right." I grab them out of her hands. "But I'm wearing my boots. No matter *what* Mom thinks of them." I toss the jeans on the bed. "Are you excited?"

"About Asuka's? We eat there at least once a week, Lily." She holds up one of my shirts, frowns, and then puts it back.

"No, about tomorrow. Finally meeting Chase Donovan. In person."

"You mean your future brother-in-law?"

I laugh. Jas has been in love with Chase since the day he came out with his first hit single. You wouldn't think it would be so hard for the top model at Laroche Cosmetics to meet a pop star, especially when they're both originally from the same small town in Texas, but Chase has been totally elusive. It'd be easier to meet the President of the United States. "Am I still the maid of honor, or has your friend Tessa taken my place?"

Jas puts her arm around me. "Not a chance, little sister. No one could ever come between you and me."

"Little?" I place my hand above her head. "I've got you beat by a good four inches. And remember, I'll be sixteen next month."

"Child," Jas says, as if seventeen and a half is so much older. She walks to the dresser and picks up Dad's picture, turning it in her hands. "Got a picture of that creep Dad's trying to keep you away from?"

"Aren't you supposed to be on *my* side?" I dig in my tote bag and retrieve Dylan's picture, wrapped in the note he gave me before I left. I hand the photo to Jas.

"Hmm. You could do so much better."

I grab the photo back. "Thanks."

"Sorry, but look at him. Grunge was over, like, *years* ago."

"Whatever." I'm sick of having to defend Dylan. I skipped school with him *one* day. It's not a felony.

Jas plops down on my bed. "How did he think he'd get away with calling your school and pretending he was Dad?"

"Wow, who told you all this, and who are you, my mother? Wait, obviously not, or you wouldn't care." I shove Dylan's picture back in my tote bag and sit down next to her. "He's a musician. Like your beloved Chase. I went with him to an audition in Houston."

"Is he nice? I mean, I hope so. Since he's totally lacking fashion sense."

I throw a pillow at her, but don't answer. He wasn't so nice when I told him I was leaving for six weeks. *At all.* I feel a knot in my stomach. I've never lied to Jas before. "It doesn't matter. Dad has effectively broken us up. At least for the summer. He even took away my cell phone."

"Harsh."

"It's not Dad's fault." I will *always* defend Dad. It was stupid, and totally not like me.

"Well, Mom never forces you to stay here any longer than you're willing to. You're *supposed* to be here six weeks every summer anyway."

"Ever occur to you that she doesn't want me here?"

"Downstairs in five!" Mom's voice crackles through the intercom system.

Jas gets up from my bed and straightens her short black skirt. "All I can say is… you need to change."

~~~

The maître d' leads us to Mom's "usual" table by the window. One of the many perks of being the great Hyacinth Laroche, CEO and Empress of Laroche Cosmetics.

Glancing around the restaurant, I *almost* understand why Mom wanted me go back and change—again. Even the waitresses are better dressed than I am. If it weren't for Jas vouching for the fact that there wasn't anything more appropriate in my entire summer wardrobe, Mom would have never let me out of the building.

I open the menu and it's obvious I'm not in Texas anymore. It's all foreign, and not just because half of it's written in Japanese. Lemongrass consommé? Where I come from, grass is for cattle. "Help me out, Jas. Order me anything that doesn't contain raw fish."

Jas rolls her eyes. "You don't know what you're missing."

I do know what I'm missing. Big open skies. Flat plains and rolling hills that go on for miles. Real food. "Surprise me. As long as it's *cooked*."

Jas closes her menu and holds it against her chest. "Just think. Chase is somewhere in the city. He could walk in here any moment." She's glowing. Like she really is going to walk down the aisle tomorrow and not just make a perfume commercial.

"Has it ever occurred to you he's probably a first-class jerk?" I hide behind my menu and pretend to be reading it to avoid Mom's glare.

"Keep your voices down, girls. Remember, the male spokesperson for *Royale pour homme* hasn't been revealed to the public yet." Mom pulls my menu down. "If word gets out, there'll be a riot at Bergdorf's tomorrow."

"Don't look at *me*. Who am I going to tell?" I flip my menu back up.

"I thought it was leaked today on purpose, Mom."

Jas wrinkles her brow.

"That was a precise leak, Jasmine. The producers of *Rise and Shine* wanted there to be a smattering of Chase's fans in the audience. Staff members' children and grandchildren." Mom lowers her voice to a whisper. "Chase's security team said we have about an hour to get him out of there after we film. Before things get out of hand."

From the way Mom says it, I could swear she's hoping it does. I knew I should have waited another week to come. I hate drama, and there will be a bucket-load of it tomorrow. I wish I didn't promise Jas I'd watch.

When our meals arrive, I hold back a snort. Jas's plate holds the tiniest piece of raw fish I've ever seen, with a little dribble of sauce over it and some greens on the side. No wonder she's so thin. She ordered me the tempura chicken and shrimp. Mom's nose wrinkles when she looks at it. I'm surprised they come to this restaurant so often, since I know Mom prefers food from her native France. As long as it's not "American" food, I guess. To this day, I have no idea how Mom and Dad ever married each other in the first place.

"I instructed Ingrid to wake us up at four, so I want you girls to go to bed as soon we get home." Mom takes a small bite out of her salmon, which I note is *not* raw, and then puts her fork down. Automatically, my mind recites one of Mom's rules: a*lways put your fork down between bites*. Mom's rules pop into my mind like sound bites. It's a curse. There's no escape.

"Four? As in *a.m.?*" My own fork clatters on my plate. That's way too early. Not to mention I'm coming from an earlier time zone. And can't she just set an alarm? Why make Ingrid get up, too?

"You have no idea what this takes, do you, Lily?" Mom sounds exasperated. "We're launching on a *live* morning show. There's no room for error. Everything has to be perfect." She pushes her plate away, having barely eaten. "The limo will pick us up at 4:30—*a.m.*—sharp. Be ready or stay home."

I look at Jas. *Stay home* sounds really good.

She grabs my hand from across the table. "I'm so glad you're here. To share this with me."

I've spent the last three years of my life avoiding this circus, and now I'm being dragged to the show. At least I'm only a spectator and not one of Mom's clowns. I squeeze her hand and smile, but I can't force out a "me, too."

It seems like only minutes before the waiter comes to take our plates. I grab the corner of mine. I'm still hungry, and there's a lot left to eat. "You've had plenty." Mom nods to the waiter. "You may take it."

"Would you like me to wrap this up, Miss?"

I shake my head. Mom doesn't believe in taking home leftovers. It's *vulgar* according to her. My eyes follow the plate as the waiter cradles it in the nook of his arm before whisking it away. I search the table for a fortune cookie—or at least a mint. There's nothing.

Mom stiffens her back and folds her napkin on the

9

table. "This perfume launch will be like no other. Every young woman will want a bottle of *Royale Princesse* after tomorrow."

Except me. Instinctively, I bring my wrist up to my nose and smell my own perfume, made from native Texas flowers. By *moi*. I quickly pretend to scratch my nose and put my hands back on my lap. I only used a drop today. I can't risk Mom getting a whiff and asking me about it. It's the last thing I'd want her to know—that there's anything about me—that's anything like her.

Two

"Fame is the perfume of heroic deeds." ~Socrates

It's not Ingrid who wakes me up in the morning; it's the lights coming on in my bedroom, followed by a cloud of Mom's perfume. I squint. She's in my closet, rifling through my clothes. I pull the sheet over my head. It's way too early to have a wardrobe war, and didn't we already establish that I have nothing else to wear? Does she think the fashion fairy came while we were sleeping last night?

She flings the closet door closed in disgust. "We leave in thirty minutes. You can put your make-up on at Bergdorf's."

Great idea, Mom. I was worried I wouldn't have time for my usual dash of lip gloss.

Twenty minutes later, I make my way to the

kitchen and find only Ingrid washing a cup and saucer at the sink. "They're waiting for you downstairs." She dries the cup and places it in the cupboard.

"Did they eat breakfast?" My stomach growls. I know Mom doesn't usually eat in the morning, but I'm hoping Jas did and there's something left I can grab.

"Jasmine wasn't feeling well. Not even a bite of toast." Ingrid's hand shakes as she folds the dish towel and sets it on the counter. "You better run, Miss Lily. Ms. Laroche is nervous this morning."

I give her arm a sympathetic pat and open the pantry. "Anything good in here?"

Ingrid pushes past me and opens a large metal bread box. She pulls out a chocolate breakfast bar and hands it to me.

"Your own private stash?" I slip it in my book bag. "I'll replace it. Thanks! And remember, you don't have to call me *Miss*."

Ingrid gives me a warning look. On my last trip I got her in trouble by forcing her to eat with me in the dining room. "Get going *Miss*." She winks at me. "This is a big day for your mother. And your sister."

I consider stalling until they leave, then remember how excited Jas was last night. I sprint toward the elevator. The power of sisterly love. I glance at the front hall clock. Four twenty-nine. Mom will be so proud of me!

As if I care.

When I get downstairs, George rushes me to the limo like there's a brush fire. I slide in across from Mom and Jas.

Mom stares at her diamond watch and lets out an enormous sigh. "Go, Curtis," she says before George even has a chance to step back on the curb.

"Morning," I mutter and settle in.

No one answers me. I'm half expecting Mom to congratulate me on my promptness, but then I remember another one of her rules: *Early is on-time, on-time is late, and late is inexcusable.* So instead, I brace for a lecture on tardiness, or at least my appearance. I get neither. She obviously has something else on her mind—Jas. Jas does *not* look good. Her skin is pale, and she's slumped against the seat.

"Jas?" I reach over and shake her knee. "Are you okay?"

Mom pushes my hand away and forces Jas to sit up. "Darling, look at me. You can't be sick. Not *now.* Whatever this is, get over it."

Whatever?

Hello?

Raw fish?

Mom curses Asuka's under her breath, threatening to sue. No need for me to bring it up.

Jas moans. Her shoulders come forward and her chest caves in. She about to launch something, all right, but it's not perfume. "Pull over... I think... I'm going to... throw up." She puts her hand over her mouth and gags.

"We can't pull over on Fifth! Where would you throw up? On the street?" Mom grabs Jasmine's hair back with one hand and sticks the other out toward me. "Lily! Your bag. Quickly!"

"What? My bag?" *You've got to be kidding me.*

"It's just an old book bag. Please, Lily. You wouldn't expect her to throw up in her Chanel, would you?"

Yes, I would, actually. Laroche Cosmetics' top model throws up in a designer handbag. What could be more perfect?

Mom gives me the look. The same one that makes every person she comes in contact with do *exactly* as she says. I dump the contents of my tote bag onto the empty seat next to me and pass it to Mom. Jasmine grabs it and vomits. Twice. In my tote.

"Curtis can throw it out when we get to Bergdorf's." Mom tucks a strand of Jasmine's hair behind her ear. "There, darling. Better?"

Jasmine shakes her head, then grabs the bag and throws up again. We need fresh air. I barely get the window down an inch before Mom yells, "Lily! The paparazzi!" and Curtis closes it from the driver's seat before I can even react.

What paparazzi? Mom *wishes* there were paparazzi, but maybe not while Jas is barfing. If we do see any, they'll be looking for Chase, not us. Even though Mom's a mega-mogul in the world of cosmetics, she's not exactly on top of the list of the most sought out celebrities, beautiful as she is.

It seems like Jas has nothing left to barf and she leans back on the seat. Mom frowns, but I think she's only worried about the perfume campaign, and not about Jas.

"Are you okay?" I dig a water bottle out of the mini-fridge and hold it out to her. "Try drinking some water."

"I can't." She shakes her head. "Sorry about your bag, sis."

"No problem," I say, but it kind of is. I liked my bag. Dad bought it for me in New Mexico and it was made by real Pueblo Indians. Mom is probably deliriously happy it's ruined because now she can finally replace it with, "something more respectable."

"What should I do with all my stuff?" I look down at the pile of clutter on the seat next to me: some colorless lip gloss, a notebook, a couple of pens, my favorite book ever, *Jane Eyre*, and my new huge copy of *The Complete Works of William Shakespeare*.

Between a few crumpled-up dollar bills and Ingrid's breakfast bar, I spot the vial of my home-made perfume. Slowly, I cover it with my hand and slide it under my leg.

"You don't need those things at Bergdorf's. There won't be any time for reading." Mom takes my bag out of Jasmine's hands, twists it, and gingerly places it on the floor of the limo as far away from her as she possibly can. Her face reveals no disgust except for a slight wrinkling of her nose and tight lips. Mom always controls her facial expressions. You never know when someone might snap a picture.

We approach Bergdorf Goodman's, and sure

enough, paparazzi are everywhere. Curtis passes the front of the store and goes around the block to the entrance on fifty-eighth. While Mom checks her appearance in her compact mirror, I slide the perfume vial into the pocket of my jeans.

Jas pulls her hoodie over her head and slips on a pair of dark sunglasses. With a little help from Mom and Curtis, she manages to climb out of the limo. "I'm fine now," she says, taking a step. "I'm just a little dizzy." She stumbles, and I grab her arm. Curtis takes her other arm, and we somehow get her to the door where we're greeted by two of Mom's "people," dressed in black from head to toe.

We're shuttled to the elevator like hostages in a rescue mission. They take us to the top floor and sweep us into Bergdorf's beauty salon, which has literally been taken over. It's swarming with black-clad, frenzied robots. The *rest* of Mom's people.

Jasmine's manager, Gaston, grabs her and flings her into a chair where her stylists are poised, ready to strike.

"*Mer…credi!*" Gaston shouts. "You look horrible!"

Jasmine groans and grabs her stomach. She pushes away a hairbrush that's hovering over her head. She gags, then gets up and staggers into the ladies' room. Without even checking to see if there's another female in the bathroom, Gaston follows her in. Mom is right behind them, wringing her hands.

Awkwardly, I look around the room. It's like

everyone's frozen in place. I smile and nod at a couple of Mom's employees, wondering what I should do.

Before I can slink away, Gaston flies out of the restroom and grabs me by the arm. "You! You will do this for your sister."

"What?" I shake my head, but he tosses me onto the stool and grabs my hair up in his hands. "A little short and way too frizzy. Maria, grab some hair extensions. Now!"

"Um…no?" My heart races. This is not happening. I try to stand but Gaston pushes me back down and keeps one hand firmly on my shoulder while he barks out orders to his crew.

Mom bursts out of the bathroom and sees me in the chair. "What in the devil is going on here? You've got to be kidding me. Isn't there another model you can call from the agency? What about the pool of models that will be in the shoot?"

"You asked for them to all be mediocre, Madame, remember? So Jasmine would outshine them?" Gaston grabs my chin. "You do not wish to keep this in the family? I know she looks plain, terrible even, but do you not trust me? I can do miracles!"

My heart beats so loudly, I think it's moved to my head. Where's the nearest exit? I am *not* doing this. No way.

Gaston holds my face in his hands. Then he runs his fingers along my cheek bones. "You are every bit as beautiful as your sister. A diamond in the rough."

As beautiful as Jas? With her smooth brown hair and startling blue eyes? Does he not see that my eyes are hazel? That my hair is what Mom calls "dirty blond," as if it's some sort of disease? That I've heard her whisper discreetly to salespeople that I'm "big-boned?" I open my mouth but nothing comes out.

"But she has no training." Mom's voice rises. "She has no idea how to pose, or walk, or speak!"

I let out a sigh of relief. Mom will tell him. I start to get out of the chair but he pushes me back down.

"She is your daughter, Madame. I'm sure she will do fine."

I think I hear Mom snort before saying, "Very well, then. Let's see what you can do."

Mom never snorts, it's so beneath her. She's always, as she would say, "decorous," so obviously she thinks I'm hideous.

Mom pivots away from us and heads back to the bathroom. I hear her muttering something in French, but I can't make out what she's saying. She's probably praying for a miracle.

"Excuse me. Um, Gaston? I'm not going to do this, okay?"

He leans down, his face only inches from mine. "You no do it for her," he whispers in his heavy French accent, tossing his head in Mom's direction. "You do it for your sister."

He whips a black cape over my T-shirt and shouts out more orders. Suddenly I'm descended upon, like vultures on a dead armadillo. I'm pulled and plucked and plastered in make-up. The hairstylist sprays my head with some sort of liquid and yanks it through my hair with a comb. Then she stretches the top part of my hair around the most gigantic rollers I've ever seen, while someone else weaves the bottom layers with long extensions that match my hair exactly.

A woman grabs my hand and shoves my fingers into a bowl of warm soapy water while another pulls off my cowboy boots and rolls up the ragged bottoms of my jeans. Tugging off my socks, she makes an audible gasp and shouts, "Pedicure. Immediately!"

"We only have another hour, people!" Gaston barks.

Another hour? How long can it possibly take? *Hurry Jas. You have to get better.*

A young man sails over to my chair and asks me to stand. He whips out a tape measure and starts assessing what seems like every inch of my body. I offer up my size, but he doesn't even acknowledge me.

Gaston stands by supervising. "A little thick for the camera, no? But she looks really good live, eh?" He turns to walk away. "But no ruffles."

I want to yell for it all to stop, but I can't seem to do it. There are too many people and I feel helpless, like I've accidently stepped on the wrong subway and it's speeding down the track, with no way to get off. Like a runaway horse.

Mom's face is almost contorted. I can tell she

doesn't know what to do with herself, which is highly unusual. I can almost see the wheels turning inside her head. Like a wind-up doll, she shuttles back and forth from my chair and the bathroom.

The rollers come out and the stylist starts teasing my hair with a comb, spraying, smoothing, teasing some more. More powder on my face. False eyelashes. Another layer of lip color. Jasmine comes slowly out of the bathroom and starts crying as soon as she sees me.

"Are you ready to come out of your cave and save me, here?" I say. "Gaston, she's back!" I get up off the stool and drag Jasmine over and help her sit down.

"Gaston!" I shriek. "She's ready! Gaston!"

He struts over to us and looks Jasmine up and down. Her eyes are bloodshot and puffy, and there's a huge red chap mark between her nose and her lips. The worst part is the smell. Worse than dead fish.

"Visine!" Gaston shouts to his assistant. Even I know it's going to take a lot more than eye drops to fix Jas now. But Gaston did say he can perform miracles, didn't he?

"Lily, you…you look gorgeous," Jas chokes out. "I… I can't get over it."

"Forget about me. We have to get you ready." I turn to Gaston. "Can I take this crap off now?"

"Of course not! And it is not as you say 'crap,' *ma cherie*. I don't know if I'll be able to transform Jasmine in time for the shoot. Go find a dress!"

The same guy who measured me drags me by the

arm to another part of the room where there's a rack of dresses lined up. He pulls dress after dress off the bar and holds them up to me, one by one, shaking his head and then tossing them to the floor. As soon as a dress hits the ground, a young woman picks it up and hangs it back on the rack. He grabs a bright yellow mini dress and holds it up against my chest, pulling it tight. "Yes! This is it. Gaston!"

Gaston floats from Jasmine to me, grunts his approval, and then tosses the dress at me. "Change, little sister, you're on!"

I look at Jas, but she's getting up from the stool and heading back to the bathroom.

My life has officially gone down the *eau de toilette.*

Three

"Happiness is a perfume you cannot pour on others

without getting a few drops on yourself."

~Ralph Waldo Emerson

I look around for a place to change, but it's obvious they expect me to put the dress on right here, in front of everyone. I pull the dress up from the bottom, over my jeans and T-shirt, and then slide the jeans off. Mr. Assistant rolls his eyes as I slip my shirt off over my head with one arm, holding the dress up with the other.

How am going to do this? I don't know the slightest thing about modeling. I despise the entire fashion industry. I think about Dylan and imagine his disapproval. He's always making fun of Mom and her hoity-toity lifestyle. And what about all the jokes he and his friends make about Chase Donovan—that he sings like a girl and has no talent? How will I ever live this down?

Dylan knows how I feel about Mom, how she broke up our family for...for...*this!* This world of make-up and fashion and stupid celebrity. And what will Dad think? That *I've* gone to the dark side, too?

Mr. Assistant zips me up and pulls the fabric down from the bottom to smooth it over my hips. He leaves me standing in front of a full length mirror and I catch my breath. I can't believe it's me. My skin is flawless, my eyes huge, my lashes dark and thick. My hair is shiny and at least twice as long, with big, soft, spiraling curls falling past my shoulders and half-way down my back. I squeeze my eyes shut and then open them again. Wow. I hate it. *I love it?*

Mom comes up behind me. "Amazing," she says, staring at my reflection like I'm some sort of mannequin in a storefront window. "Absolutely amazing. Do you finally get it now, Lily? What I've been telling you all these years? What a shame."

I wonder what shame she's referring to, but decide to remain silent. My goal in life is to speak to her only when necessary. As far as I'm concerned, she stopped being my mother three years ago. And the funny thing is, she doesn't even seem to notice.

Gaston joins us at the mirror. "I told you, yes? Your younger daughter is gorgeous, Madame. Stunning. Notice how the eye shadow we chose brings out the green in her eyes. She's...*magnifique!*" He folds his arms in front of his chest, looking smug.

"Yes, she is. Good work, Gaston. But the question now is whether she can pull this off. Get her over to the photographer and director immediately. We're starting from scratch here."

Mr. Assistant is given instructions in French. I assume they're about what to do with me next. As he escorts me out of the dressing area, Mom leans in and whispers in my ear, "Don't mess this up, Lily." I feel like running through the doors and down the escalator. Onto Fifth Avenue. All the way to Texas. But I go with Gaston's assistant. One foot in front of the other.

I glance back at the bathroom door, but there's no sign of Jas. Is she that sick? I'll do this *one* time for her, and that's it. I sigh and resign myself to this horrible fate. Dad will understand, won't he? And he of all people should know that once Mom makes a decree, there's no changing her mind.

We take the elevator down to the staging area and Mr. Assistant leads me to the set. I turn to ask him what I'm supposed to do next, but he disappears into the elevator and leaves me standing there, like an idiot. I search for the nearest exit, in case I need to make an emergency escape, and that's when I first see him.

Chase Donovan.

In person.

Gulp.

I've always prided myself on not being one of those star-struck kind of girls. I don't put posters of boys up in my room. I don't read magazines that describe every move they make or fill out quizzes to see if we'd be compatible. But when I see Chase, I suck in my breath. It's not totally lost on me that every teenage girl in America—and half the rest of the world—would do anything to be me right now. I pray my mouth will work, and I'll actually be able to speak. I tell myself he must be a jerk. Has to be, right? But what an adorable jerk.

He's wearing gray dress pants and a button-down, white fitted shirt. His dark blond hair is thick and curls just enough to keep it out of his eyes. He glances over at me and I want to look away fast. But I don't. Because even from where I'm standing, I can see his eyes are the color of the sea in Greece, where we vacationed last summer. Not the aqua color of the shallow part when the sun shines on it, but the dark blue of the deeper water. I stare, embarrassed, but unable to look away.

Jerk! Jerk, Jerk!

Of course I have no *proof* that Chase is a jerk. And he *is* a Texan, so how bad can he be? According to Jas—and all those tabloids she reads—he's supposedly "unaffected by his fame." Yeah, right. I bet that's garbage.

And how can Jas be in love with someone she doesn't even know? It's ridiculous. Her room in Texas remains exactly like the day she left, including posters of Chase on every wall. And even though she's too cool to put his picture up in her new chic Manhattan bedroom, she hasn't changed a bit. She's *obsessed.*

I love my sister, but what girl plans her nuptials when she's only seventeen, and worse, with a boy she's never even met? But that's the way Jas is. It's a page right out of Mom's playbook: decide what you want out of life and then go for it with all you've got. Don't let anything stop you. Even if it means leaving one of your daughters behind.

While I try not to bore holes into Chase, Mom appears and introduces me to a nice-looking woman wearing a bright red pants suit, who turns out to be Chase's mom. Like the hypocrite she is, Mom puts her arm around me affectionately, smiling wide. "Betty, this is my daughter, *Lily.*"

"It's a pleasure to meet you, dear," Betty says, with a strong Texas drawl. She holds out her hand.

I take it and squeeze gently for a moment before letting go. "The pleasure's mine." My voice sounds like it's coming from somewhere else. I guess all the years of Mom's training before she deserted me are in there somewhere.

"I didn't realize you had another daughter, Hya," Betty says to Mom.

No surprise there.

Mom just smiles without showing any teeth.

Betty places her hand on my forearm. "Have you met Chase yet, darlin'?"

"Not yet." *I've only been ogling him from afar.* I wobble a little in my heels and glance his way.

Chase approaches us, and then leans down and kisses his mom's cheek. Betty is smiling from ear to ear. She turns to me. "Lily, I'd like you to meet my son,

Chase."

Chase holds his hand out, and I give him mine, praying it's not too sweaty. His hand is warm and strong. I manage a weak "hey." Chase grins with this adorable smile, and I feel like I need to slap myself across the face. I am close to becoming a mumbling fool. He is *so* cute.

"There's been a change of plans," Mom tells them. "Lily will be working with Chase today. My daughter Jasmine is a little under the weather."

"I'm sorry Jasmine isn't feeling well." Chase looks right at me and smiles. "But lucky me."

Normally, I'd think: What a line, what a creep. But the way he says it is friendly—almost like he's trying to assure me it's okay.

"What will this mean for the ad campaign?" Mrs. Donovan asks.

"Well, it's a shame, but I'm afraid Lily will have to take Jasmine's place now in *all* of the ads. As you know, we'll be live, and this is a storybook campaign. We can't very well have our hero switching heroines after the first shoot."

What? No way! I can't breathe.

Mom looks disappointed, but keeps her expression even. "We have about forty minutes before we're on. Please, follow me, and we'll go over everything again with the director." She leads us to a back room lounge where we meet with the crew. I try to get Mom alone to tell her that this is *not* going to work, but she's too busy bossing everyone around—including me.

Jas told me all about this enormous "storybook" plan that Mom and her advertising team came up with for the new perfume. I didn't pay much attention—since it didn't involve me—but I heard enough to be scared. Really scared.

I know the first shoot will be here—today—live, thanks to Mom's connection with the producers of *Rise and Shine*, the country's most popular morning show. Then the ad campaign will develop like a love story.

The public will be cordoned off and held at a distance, and the entire spectacle will be filmed live. Mom's new perfumes will be on top of the piano, hidden in a jewel-encrusted royal coffer. Chase will stand up and pull a girl from the group—Jasmine—now me—and sing the rest of the song, looking into her eyes. He will lead this girl—gulp—me, to the piano, where I will sit with him until he finishes the song. Then, finally, the perfumes will be revealed.

Mom's team will make a commercial out of the entire scene and run it for a couple of weeks. Then, every so often, Chase and his new dream girl...um...me, will show up in beautiful places all over the world and be filmed in romantic scenes advertising *Royale* Perfume. I think the next stop is the Eiffel Tower. Not what I had planned for my summer vacation. I haven't been to France since Meme died when I was twelve, and I decided then that I was never going back. Being with Mom is nauseating enough in New York, but it's utterly horrifying in Paris.

The director goes over the instructions again. "Is everything clear, Lily?" Mom asks. I nod my head. For reasons of secrecy, there have been no rehearsals, no previous photo shoots. The idea is to make it resemble reality TV as much as possible. That part should be easy. Since I've never modeled, or acted, it will definitely be like a reality show. *Punk'd* is the one I'm thinking of. I pray Jasmine will walk in the door any moment, all dressed and ready to go. *Please, please, please!*

When the director is done prepping us, I whisper in Mom's ear, "Is Jasmine better, yet?" My voice quivers.

"Believe me, Lily, I wish she were, even more than you do. She's still very ill. You are going to have to do this. Pull yourself together."

The doors swing open, and one of the black-clad robots yells that the models have arrived. Robot Man takes me back to the set and tells me to go stand in the middle of the throng. "Five minutes," he hollers.

I make my way to the middle of the group, remembering Mom had ordered twenty "mediocre" models, none to be as pretty as Jas. Am I pretty enough to stand out in the crowd? I find a place to stand in the center of these "not quite good enough" girls and wonder if any of them know how they were chosen for this gig, and would they even care? A tall redhead in a blue dress eyes me up and down, then turns away.

"That's a pretty dress," I say, which I know sounds totally lame. She doesn't hear me, or pretends not to. I take a peek at her face to see if I can spot any obvious flaws. Nope. She looks perfectly fine to me.

I shift from foot to foot, painfully aware of the stilettos I'm wearing. I guess Mom didn't consider that I'm likely to fall flat on my face. Sure, I look different on the outside, but did she forget it's still me on the inside?

Chase and Mom wait in the back room, not to be seen until the very last moment. When Chase's fans arrive, I am grateful for the anonymity of being a nobody. Even before he appears, girls are screaming in decibels I've never heard before. The crowd consists of mostly pre-teens and their mothers. I wonder if Mom's catering to the wrong clientele. It appears that most of Chase's fans aren't even old enough to wear Mom's kind of perfume. But this is a publicity stunt. *Royale* perfumes will be world famous from the moment Chase lifts the bottles from the chest.

Finally, Chase is escorted to the piano, and the screaming intensifies. He sits down on the bench and gives a quick wave to a group of three girls who are holding up a hand-made sign that says, "We love you Chase!" in hot-pink glitter. They squeal, and one of them wipes away a tear. *How pathetic.*

A trio of musicians plays back up music while Chase briefly searches the gaggle of models in front of him. Is it possible he won't recognize me after having only met me minutes before? I scan the models again. I'm the only one wearing a yellow dress.

I think he's spotted me, but he doesn't maintain eye contact. With his eyes half-closed, he plays an intro, and then starts to sing. I've heard his songs a million times on the radio, but I am struck by the beauty of his voice in person. I take a deep breath and focus on the job at hand, which is to try to appear like I'm falling in love. I'm surprised how easy it is to do, and partially sickened by it. I had *so* thought I was better than this.

Chase is singing a love song, of course, but I find it hard to concentrate on the words. I know in a moment he'll be coming for me. And then the whole world, well it seems like the whole world, will see me. On live television.

A few of the models are swaying softly to the music. I try to act natural and do the same. Then I do what I was told explicitly *not* to do—look directly at a camera. I quickly look away in fear. I bump into the red-headed girl and almost fall, just barely catching myself at the last second. What am I doing? What have I willingly gone along with? I start to sweat and feel my face grow hot.

I repeat in my head the instructions the director gave me. *"Just stand there looking pretty. When Chase grabs your hand, follow him and sit at the piano."* Simple. There are no speaking parts. I've got this.

The moment arrives and I see Chase rise from the bench. He grabs the microphone off the stand and keeps on singing. The crowd of models parts like the Red Sea until I'm alone, standing directly in front of him, my knees wobbling. Fainting would not be good right now. Chase's new girlfriend should not be a moron.

Chase is totally cool and composed. He smiles

ever so slightly and gives me a reassuring look as he walks toward me holding out his free hand. Singing the lyrics directly to me, he doesn't miss a note. I can't distinguish a single word. The entire room is blurry. My heart bangs like a drum in my ears and I feel light-headed. Focus. You're almost there. I take a step in his direction and my legs tremble. Finally, our hands touch, and I think I'll be okay. I wobble slightly but regain my footing. Breathe.

Chase leads me to the piano, and I sit down beside him, grateful to be off my feet. I made it. Now nothing can go wrong. He opens the lid of the coffer and pulls out two, huge, crown-shaped bottles, one at a time. He sets the first one on top of the piano, and then hands the other one to me, a look of adoration on his angelic face. What am I supposed to do now? I don't remember this part of the instructions and draw a total blank. I pull the stopper from the bottle and dab some perfume on my finger. I reach up and touch it to his neck, just below his ear. I hear a collective gasp from Mom's peeps. Something's wrong. I look at the other bottle that's still on top of the piano. It's shaped like a crown that a king would wear, more masculine than the one I have in my hand. I recognize the word *homme* written on it and realize, even with my rapidly declining French, that I have just doused Chase with *Royale Princesse*. For girls.

I freeze in terror. Chase will hate me. I've just damaged his masculinity in front of the whole world.

Chase takes my hand and touches it to my cheek.

"I've got my own," he whispers. There wasn't supposed to be any talking. Only the song. Not knowing what to do next, I hand him the dark amber men's crown from on top of the piano. He opens the men's perfume and the heavy scent of *Royale pour homme* mixed with the flowery scent of *Royale Princesse* nauseates me. I fight an impulse to gag.

Chase dabs a little of the men's perfume on his collar bone, and then touches my neck, too. Now we're even. His hand moves from my neck to my face and suddenly he is lifting my chin. He leans down and brushes my lips with his. The little girls in the audience scream at a fever pitch. It's the briefest of kisses, if you can even call it that, but my heart beats erratically. A kiss was *not* in the script! *How dare he?* I hope the heavy layer of make-up will cover the blush I feel creeping across my cheeks.

Suddenly it's all over, and Chase stands up. He takes my hand and helps me to my feet. We stand by the piano while the crowd goes wild.

Then we walk over to the crowd of teeny boppers. They're literally ready to faint when Chase touches them. Normally, I'd think this was pathetic, but now I know how they feel. I am so disappointed in *moi!*

The young girls treat me like the Cinderella character who walks around Disney World. They have no idea I'm a nobody and keep asking for my autograph. One of Mom's workers hands us both pens. I scribble "Lily" on everything from paper to a pink baseball cap. One girl wants me to sign her arm with a permanent marker. I look up at Chase to get his opinion, raising my eyebrows.

"Hey!" he says to the little girl. "What's up?" He gives her a high five and I think she's about to keel over. Tears stream down her freckled face and she can't stop hiccupping. "Would you like Lily to sign *this* for you instead?" He pulls a crisp white handkerchief out of his pants pocket, like he's pulling a rabbit out of a hat. The girl nods her head furiously. She's speechless.

"You can use my back," he says to me, handing me the handkerchief. I fold it into thirds, afraid the ink will seep into his shirt, and sign *Lily* with as much flourish as I can muster. My hands shake. Why am I the one signing the handkerchief and not Mr. Pop Star?

"May I sign it also?" Chase asks the little girl in a humble voice. I want to giggle. Again she nods, and a new stream of tears falls.

"Lily..." He motions for me to turn around.

I take a deep breath and turn. My dress is strapless and I feel his hand brush my skin as he moves my hair out of the way. He signs the handkerchief and then leans down to the little girl's height. He gives it to her along with a hug.

Okay, that was sweet. I can almost believe he *is* a nice guy. But what about that kiss? I should be furious. I know it wasn't a real kiss, but he had no right. My cheeks feel hot again.

One of Chase's bodyguards leans in behind us. "It's time to stop autographing. We need to get you out of here."

Chase looks across the line of fans we haven't got to yet and shakes his head. "Not yet. We need to see all of them." He grins at his bodyguard. "Please…"

The bodyguard sighs, but nods his head. "Speed it up."

Chase doesn't stop until every last fan has been touched, and every last autograph request has been fulfilled. Finally, we're practically dragged away by Chase's security team and led back to the lounge.

As soon as we enter, I see Mom in one corner discussing the tape with the director. Chase's mom is sitting on the leather couch sipping tea from a cup, deep in conversation with Jas, who still looks pale. Mom looks at me out of the corner of her eye, and I'm terrified. I wonder how she'll handle my mix-up. I'm glad for all the extra people in the room, especially Mrs. Donovan. Mom will have to be nice to me in front of her.

Chase puts one hand on the small of my back and escorts me to a chair. I want to make a wisecrack about the shoot being over now, but bite my tongue. One of Mom's crew asks both of us what we would like to drink. No one has ever asked *me* that before, even when I've gone with Jasmine to some of her shoots.

"I'll get it, thank you." I grab a bottle of water from the beverage table and drink directly from it, no glass. I purposely look at Mom, who grimaces. I still have some fight left in me for our passive-aggressive war. I kick off the stilettos. My senses are finally returning. Now, if I don't actually look at Chase, and just focus on what he did at the piano, I'll be back to normal. And Chase will go back to being the jerk I thought he was.

"Lily, that was spectacular. When did you come up with that clever idea to put the woman's perfume on Chase?" Mrs. Donovan asks.

I almost choke on my water. Is she being sarcastic?

"You were great," Jas says to me. I can hear the pain in her voice.

Mrs. Donovan sets her cup down. "Chase, come and meet Lily's sister, Jasmine. The two of you have so much in common."

What would that be? The love of fame and fortune?

Chase takes a glass of ice water from one of the servers and kindly thanks him. *Phony.* Jasmine starts to stand up, but Chase puts his hand out. "Please. Don't get up." He looks concerned. "How are you feeling?"

Is he disappointed now that he's seen her? Even after barfing all morning, she still looks beautiful.

Jasmine flashes Chase her prettiest smile. "It was just a case of food poisoning, I think. Bad sushi. I feel much better now."

Why couldn't she have felt much better two hours ago?

Mrs. Donovan slides over on the sofa so Chase has room to sit between them. Perfect. Let's get the attention off of me and onto Jas.

Chase smiles back at her. "That's why I never eat the stuff."

That's my cue. "I'm going to go change." I make my way toward the door.

"Not so fast, Lily," the art director yells my way. "Now we do the still shots. At the studio."

I roll my eyes and plop down in the chair farthest away from everyone. How did I ever let this happen to me? My life hasn't just gone down the toilet—it's ruined.

Drowned in the stench of *Royale Princesse.*

Four

"I felt something so intense, I could only express it in a perfume." ~ Jacques Guerlain

"Give me a starting position, please," the photographer barks. "Forward facing."

"Huh?" I look at Jas. I feel like a complete fool. Chase stands comfortably in front of the camera like a pro. I try to arrange myself next to him, but it's not working.

"Right foot twelve o'clock, left foot ten," Jas says, striking a pose.

What? I point one toe toward the camera and turn my body to the side.

"Shoulders back!" The photographer snarls. "You're slouching. And remember your face."

Jas ignores the photographer and speaks directly

to me. "It's okay, Lily. Take a deep breath. A good picture begins in your mind. You have to be an actress."

I try to imagine I'm Jasmine and copy her pose. The photographer looks through his lens and groans. Mom is quiet but flashes me her evil eye every time I'm dumb enough to look her way.

"Give us a minute," Jas says to the photographer.

She leads me a few feet away from the set. Grabbing both my arms, she stares at me. "Listen. Remember when we were little and used to goof around dressing up like princesses and pretending there was an imaginary prince? You need to get back there in your mind. Create a fantasy. Whatever you are thinking on the inside, shows up on the outside."

I nod my head, even though Jas was the one who forced me to play dress up, and I never did get into it like she did. My fantasy was to be Fern in *Charlotte's Web* and have my own pet pig named Wilbur. I hated to dress up then, and I still do. But now is not the time to confess.

Jas pats me on the back. "Think to yourself, 'I am beautiful. Chase adores me. We are in love. I am gorgeous and happy.' Got it?"

I nod my head again and go back to my place. Chase has been quiet and patient, but I think I see a tiny smirk on his face when I return. He's standing behind me and puts one hand on my waist like the photographer instructs. He leans down and whispers in my ear, "Pretend I'm not here, like this is just any other shoot."

"This is not about you! I've never done this

before," I hiss.

He chuckles softly and the camera flashes. I can see the shot in my mind, me angry and him laughing.

"Think happy thoughts," he whispers.

"Good idea," I say. "I'll just imagine you're Dylan."

"Who's Dylan?"

"My boyfriend," I say smugly. I don't know why I'm being mean to Chase, but I don't want him to think I'm messing up because he's Mr. Heartthrob. I try to picture Dylan but his memory has gone sour. I don't want to admit that Chase has already blotted him almost entirely from my mind. I decide to take Jasmine's advice and pretend I'm a beautiful princess and Chase loves me.

"Much better," the photographer says. *Click.* "Good." *Click.* "Now turn your head slightly to the side. Beautiful." *Click.*

The photographer is on a roll. "I want a head shot of what you did at the piano," he says. "Lily, hold the perfume bottle and pretend to put some on Chase's neck."

There's no missing the smirk on Chase's face this time. "You just had to touch my neck back there at Bergdorf's, didn't you?"

"I couldn't remember what I was supposed to do."

"Sure."

We're facing each other now and his nearness makes me feel warm. I'm forced to look at his adorable face. I try not to look into his dark blue eyes because I already know their hypnotic effect. What's wrong with me? He's not my type. I go back to my jerk mantra. I start making a list of all the reasons I shouldn't like him.

Number one, my sister is madly in love with him. Number two, he probably already has a girlfriend. Number three, I don't like blonds. Number four, he'd never like me back. Ouch. That one hurts. Number five, I hate celebrities. *That* one shakes some sense into me. He's part of Mom's world. Her messed-up, shallow, miserable world.

"Let's just get this over with," I say.

"Wow, you really don't like me, do you?" Chase's eyebrows scrunch up. Even that looks cute.

"I don't *know* you, Chase." It comes out harsh, so I try to explain. "I'm not into this stuff, okay? My sister's the model, not me. I got roped into this."

"Sorry," Chase whispers.

"Ahem." The photographer waits for us to stop talking. "One more. Turn a little toward the camera." Click. "Good." Click. "Last one." Click. Click. "Okay, we're done. That's a wrap."

I look at Gaston, who's ordered make-up added to my face every half-hour, all day long. "Are we done? Can I take this stuff off now?"

Mom answers for him. "Please Lily, you can take your make-up off at home. There are still paparazzi outside."

I roll my eyes. As if I care about the paparazzi. All I want is my face back. My boots. My jeans and T-shirt. I look for my Indian bag but then remember Jasmine barfed in it. "Where are my clothes?" Mom probably threw them away while we were still at Bergdorf's.

Jasmine grabs her giant Juicy tote bag and pulls out my old jeans and shirt. "Here."

"Thanks," I say and then mumble to everyone, "It was nice meeting you." Grabbing my clothes I head for the dressing room.

"You can keep that dress," Mom calls out cheerfully. "It's one of the perks of being a working girl."

Working girl? I roll my eyes again and shake my head. Please let them leave while I'm changing so I can go straight to the car with Curtis.

When I get in the dressing room, I look at myself one last time in the mirror. The smoky make-up around my eyes makes them look huge. I examine the hair extensions and decide they're not something I should attempt to remove myself.

I peel off the yellow dress and put on my clothes. A T-shirt and jeans have never felt so good. I feel my pocket and sigh with relief. The perfume vial is still there. How could I have been so careless?

My boots are missing, but I refuse to put the stilettos back on. I roll them up inside the dress and go out barefoot. Everyone is still talking. Chase and Jas are laughing like they've known each other for years.

"Lily, come here." Jas waves me over. She puts her hand on Chase's arm and smiles up at him. Jas has always had a way with guys. I wish I had her confidence, but I guess when it came to Dylan, I didn't need any. He pursued me.

"Chase's band is going out tonight after the launch party," Jas says. "They don't get to the city very often. He wants to know if we'll go with them."

Has she forgotten I'm only fifteen years old? I'll be sixteen in a couple of weeks, but still. Wasn't that the main reason Dad separated me from Dylan, because he turned eighteen this summer—and he's in a rock band? And if I remember right, Jas has a big heart circling Chase's birthday in December on her calendar, and then he'll be eighteen, too. And who knows how old the other two guys in his band are. I don't even know their names. Does anyone? It seems like they only exist to frame Chase when he's singing.

"I'm kind of tired, Jas…"

Her eyes get big and she arches her eyebrows, like she'll kill me if I say no. "Just for a little while?" she asks in her sweetest voice. Like with everything else today, I'm trapped. It wouldn't look right for her to go alone. She probably thinks I owe her, but in my opinion, she owes me.

"You might want to wear shoes, though," Chase says looking down at my feet. Suddenly I'm grateful for that pedicure I got at Bergdorf's. Is he criticizing me, or just making small talk?

"I wear cowboy boots, like all good Texans do," I say. "You got a problem with that?"

"Not at all, I might wear some myself."

Jasmine seems to think she needs to make excuses for me. "My sister still lives in Texas. She's just here for the summer." In case that wasn't enough she adds, "She rides horses."

"Well, that explains everything." Chase winks at me. I hate when guys wink, but Chase doesn't do it in the yucky way some guys do. I can tell he's just teasing me.

"Dylan might not approve," Chase continues.

I'm so afraid Jasmine will blow my cover and expose my true relationship with Dylan, or lack thereof, but she merely raises her eyebrows.

"Oh, Dylan won't mind," she replies for me. I should've known she'd play along. It's to her advantage for Chase to believe I have a boyfriend. And I do... sort of. The last thing Dylan said in his letter was that he would wait for me.

I remind myself how long Jas has dreamt of this moment. Her chance to meet Chase, to go out with him. She has to be devastated about the ad campaign. But at least I'm making myself as unattractive as possible to Chase, and besides, no one has *ever* preferred me over Jas.

"Of course she'll go." Jas laughs. "We'll sneak out of the party around ten and meet you at *Ciao*." She glances at me after she says it, threatening me with her baby blues.

Ciao? That club Jas warned me she would drag me to before I even left Texas? Where they allow certain underage people— i.e., celebrity or inheritance kids—to dance but supposedly not drink? I told her there was no way I'd go. I can't think of anywhere I would rather *not* be. I bite my lip. This will be my final sacrifice.

Jas and Chase finalize our plans while I shove the yellow dress and the stilettos in Jas's bag and look for my boots. "They're not there," Jas says, apparently reading my mind. "I have no idea what Mom did with them."

I turn to leave, but Mom grabs my arm and whispers in my ear, "Walk out that door barefoot, and you'll never see your precious Texas again."

Jas gives me a sympathetic look and hands me back the stilettos. They feel much worse the second time around, but I wear them anyway, and limp out of the studio.

When we get outside, we're greeted by a herd of vultures, a.k.a. the *pap*. Cameras flash everywhere. "Where've you been hiding your youngest daughter, Hya?" one guy shouts at Mom. Cool as ever, Mom smiles in his direction without saying a word. I can see her gloating as she slides into the limo.

Five

"A perfume, it is like a new dress. It returns to you quite simply marvelous." ~ Estée Lauder

As soon as we're home, I go straight to my room and crash on my bed. I wonder if Dylan saw the show and what he thinks of me if he did. It was a morning program, and he sleeps till at least noon, but someone will tell him. Like any minute now, I'm sure. I have to find a way to contact him. Let him know it wasn't my fault.

The picture of Dad on the dresser makes me feel even worse. My heart aches at the thought of him seeing me in one of Mom's commercials. I take the vial of my homemade perfume out of my pocket and roll it between my fingers. I feel like pouring it down the sink. I am *not* like them. I will *never* be like them.

"Lily, come down." It's Mom on the intercom.

"We're going to watch the tape from Bergdorf's." I don't answer. I want to say no, but my curiosity gets the best of me. I mean, who wouldn't want to see themselves on TV?

When I get downstairs to the family room, Mom and Jas are waiting for me with the TV paused. Jas cries as we watch the tape five or six times. The first time we get to the part on the piano bench, Mom gasps as if it's just happening now. "What were you thinking, Lily, putting women's perfume on Chase?"

"I couldn't remember what to do. I thought it was his."

"You two look like you're actually in love." Jas laughs through her tears. "You did a great job acting."

"That expression you see on my face is not love— it's panic. They must look similar on tape." I cringe. If Jas had any idea how bad I'm crushing on Chase, she'd flip.

Mom turns to me. "Listen very carefully, Lily. I've worked a long time on this advertising campaign, and you are not going to blow it. Do you have any idea how hard it was to get Chase Donovan? Nearly impossible." She stares at me with wild eyes. She's the only person I've ever seen whose eyes look almost lavender. I'm sometimes startled by my own mother's beauty, even though I've been looking at her my whole life.

"Luckily for us," Mom continues, "Chase's mother still manages his career, and she adores my neck cream, and my perfume. We need to make the best of this situation."

The entire thing is so unfair, but I know better

than to talk back to Mom when she's this passionate about something. Dad learned that the hard way when she decided she couldn't live in Texas anymore. She needed the city, needed to travel back and forth to her beloved Paris whenever she felt compelled. He'd married a girl who said it didn't matter where they lived, as long as she could build her career in make-up. She lied.

"Your appearance in public is more important than ever now. For the time being, you *are* Chase Donovan's girlfriend. Act accordingly." Mom stands in front of me and dares me to defy her. "That means hair, make-up, and clothing. At all times. Do you have any idea what fell into your lap today? Make something out of it."

"Are we done?" I meet her eyes. I can't fight her on this, but she'll know how much I despise every minute. Jas sits on the couch looking at me like I'm some sort of alien.

"You are dismissed," Mom says. "Jasmine, see if you can find Lily something decent to wear tonight to the launch party."

Fuming, I turn and leave the room. I'm stuck. And worse, I hate to admit there's a part of me that would do anything to see Chase again, anything to feel those lips brush mine, even if it's just to sell perfume. I conjure up Dylan's face, but it has the opposite effect I'm looking for. Instead, I think about Fire Star and imagine I'm galloping her across the prairie. That's where I belong. Not here. Not with Chase Donovan.

Jas follows me upstairs. Before today, I wasn't

even going to the launch party. I don't see how anything she owns will fit me. Still, I let her drag me into her giant closet and sit me down on the large round ottoman in the middle.

"I've got tons of clothes left over from jobs. I'm sure we'll find you something." She starts rifling through her closet. "It won't matter that you're taller if it's a dress."

"Hey, let me use your cell phone." I hold out my hand. "I need to call Dylan before he hears about this from someone else."

"I'm sure it's too late for that." Jasmine tosses me her phone anyway. "Hurry up. I want you to try this on." She holds up a tiny piece of shiny silver fabric on a hanger that I assume is a dress.

"Um, no." I shake my head. I dial Dylan's cell and get his voicemail. I think about leaving him a message but decide to hang up. Even though he won't recognize the number, the area code will tip him off. Should I call Dad? I want to, but I just can't. I give Jasmine back her phone. "No answer."

"Good. Don't tell Mom I let you use it."

"Yeah, like I'm going to tell Mom." I roll my eyes. I get up and peruse Jas's dresses, pulling out a feminine one with pretty blue flowers on it. "How about this?" It's totally not my style, but I don't see any better options.

"Oh my gosh, Lily, no! Give me that." She tosses it to the floor. "That's hideous. It reminds me of the bluebonnet fields back home."

"What's wrong with bluebonnets?" I slump back down on the ottoman. I used them to make my perfume, along with yellow roses. "And you just called Texas home. Don't you miss it?"

"I could never go back. To live, I mean. It's so boring. New York is home now." She holds up a short, elegant white gown. "This Armani would look great on you."

"Isn't that too fancy?"

"Hardly." She holds it against herself and looks in the full length mirror. "I wore it to a premiere a few months ago, but no one will remember." She turns from side to side. "I love it!"

"What about shoes?" My feet are a whole size and a half bigger than Jasmine's—and Mom's.

"Those silver Louboutins you wore today will be perfect."

I moan.

"Here, try it."

I put the dress on and stand in front of the mirror. The white fabric seems to glow in the light of the crystal chandelier that shines above our heads. It is pretty.

"Wow. You look stunning." Jas laughs. "You just better stay away from Chase. Remember, he's *mine*."

"Don't worry about that." I laugh back. But I am worried. Very worried.

Suddenly, Mom's voice booms through the intercom. "Girls, Gaston is here. He brought Samantha to do your make-up."

Are you kidding me? What *is* it with these people and their make-up?

Jas pushes the button. "Send them up!"

"I don't want to do this, Jas. I hate this."

"I don't get you." Jas grabs me by my bare shoulders and shakes me. "Are you sure you're my sister?" She looks me in the eyes. "Relax, have some fun!"

"I just want to go home. To Texas." I flop back down.

Gaston pokes his head in the closet. "*Bonsoir!*"

Resume nightmare.

Act Two.

Six

A woman should wear fragrance wherever she expects to be kissed." ~Coco Chanel

𝓘'm really not much of a party person. I'd rather be alone, or with animals. When I ride Fire Star far from the ranch to the open land, where there's no one around for miles, I feel free, and happy. The solitude exhilarates me. Ever since I came to New York, I feel like I'm suffocating. Even in my own room, I sense people everywhere, closing in.

When we get to the launch party, that feeling intensifies. Jas drags me to the dance floor with a group of her friends who frankly, I can't stand. Before tonight, they barely acknowledged my existence. Jas's BFF Tessa is the most annoying of all. She puts one arm around me and the other around Jas and tries to dance in this uncomfortable human chain. I put on a fake, half smile and move my feet back and forth, planning my escape.

"I love that dress," Tessa gushes over me. "Didn't Jazzy wear that to… oh gosh… I mean, I won't mention it."

"I don't really care," I say.

Tessa tips her head back and laughs. Hard. "You're so funny!"

Yeah, a real riot.

"I'm going to go get something to drink," I shout over the music.

"I'll go with her," Tessa says to the group, as if I need a designated escort.

I look at her like she's crazy, but quickly change my expression. "No, that's okay. I'm fine. I'll be right back."

I leave fast, hoping no one follows me. I'm not ten feet away before Curtis has my arm. "Hya wants you. Now." Curtis is not only our driver, but as far as I can tell, Mom's ultimate personal assistant. He's never more than a few steps away. I wonder how much he gets paid for that, and if it could possibly be worth it.

Mom's talking to a bald, older man wearing one of those silk dinner jacket things that looks like pajamas. Gag.

"Frankie, this is my daughter, Lily." Mom rests her hand affectionately on my forearm. Gag again. And who over the age of ten would still let people call them *Frankie*?

"Lily, this is *Frankie Shores*." Mom says it like I should know who he is. I don't. She probably senses that I'm clueless, so she adds, "As you know, he directed that movie you girls love, *Full Moon*." Never heard of it! Luckily, I don't have to comment. It's enough to just smile and hold out my hand. Everyone here prefers to hear their own voice anyway.

"It's a pleasure to meet you, darling." Frankie grabs my fingers and doesn't let go. He kisses both my cheeks. "Your mother has told me so much about you."

That's interesting. My mother doesn't *know* anything about me. "Nice to meet you," I say, and contemplate how to extricate my hand from his corpulent clutches. The gold hoop earrings he's wearing makes him look like a short, glamorized Mr. Clean.

"Lily, it's time for us to go to a private room for awhile. Chase is there." Mom smiles with her mouth closed. "Mr. Shores will join us."

"What about Jas?" I glance back at the dance floor, suddenly wishing I was still there. Even Tessa would be better company than Mom and Frankie Shores. And Chase? My heart beats faster at the thought of seeing him again. I feel like I'm betraying Jas if she's not with me.

"Curtis will bring her in a moment." Mom puts her hand on my back and I find myself following one of her black-clad people with an earpiece out into the hallway. We walk quickly to another private gathering with a handful of other guests.

When I enter the room, I am blown away by the

beauty. Mom, who loves flowers above all else—except maybe fortune and fame—has ordered mountains of yellow, orange, and cream colored roses. They're everywhere, except on Mom's own private table. There she has only hyacinths. Giant purple hyacinths.

The room makes me think of Meme, my French grandmother, who loved flowers as much as Mom and I do, which is why she named Mom, Hyacinth, and why Mom named Jasmine and me after flowers, too.

I see Chase in the back of the room, deep in conversation with a group of pretty girls. Are they part of his entourage? His harem, maybe? Mom spent years instructing Jas and me, since we were too young to care, how to properly behave with boys. It's been drilled into my head to never approach a guy first. I'm relieved to fall back on my training and ignore Chase's presence altogether. I focus on the conversation Mom and Mr. Shores are doing their best to include me in.

"Have you ever considered acting?" Mr. Shores asks.

"Uh...no." Mom hates when I give short answers, but I don't think "not in a million years" would be appropriate, and I can't think of anything else to say. I look back in Chase's direction, but no longer see him. *Stop looking!*

Suddenly, I feel someone touch my arm. I don't have to turn to know who it is.

"Hi, Lily."

The minute I hear his voice, I melt like ice in a

glass of sweet tea on a hot summer's day. Is it okay if I just put my head on his shoulder right now and close my eyes? What's wrong with me?

I turn to face him. He leans down, pecks my cheek, and then hugs me. I hug him back. A little hug can't hurt, right? But surprisingly, it does. I don't want to let go. This has to be imaginary. He's a pop star, and I'm not above the pull like I thought I was. But he doesn't have to know how I feel. I can fight this.

I take a deep breath. "Hello, Chase. Enjoying the party?"

"Very much. Where's your sister?"

"She should be here somewhere." I look away. I don't want to notice his cute, slightly messy hair. The dimples that form when he smiles. The sincere look in his eyes. Must. Stop. Now. "I'll go find her," I say, turning to leave.

Mom's arm comes out like a whip. She grabs mine, giving it a hard squeeze. "Don't be silly. Curtis will bring her shortly."

Chase kisses Mom on the cheek and shakes Mr. Shore's hand. Frankie boy looks like a Rottweiler eyeing up a steak. I guess Chase is everyone's ticket. A perfume ad. A movie. Whatever he touches is golden. I've never seen Mom so proud of herself.

"Nice to see you again, Chase. How's the tour going?" Frankie tightens the silk belt of his dinner jacket, and I get ready for another boring conversation about the "biz."

"Great. We play at Madison Square Garden tomorrow night." Chase turns to me. "Lily, do you and Jasmine have any plans? You could be my VIP guests at the show."

Not happening. And besides, what makes him think I'd even *want* to go to his concert? I try to think of a good response, but Mom answers for me. "That would be wonderful, Chase. The girls are free tomorrow night. I'm sure they'd love to join you."

Chase looks at me and I glare back. I will not let him think I'm at his beck and call. I know I should go to the stupid concert for Jasmine's sake, but I'm not happy about it. How could I lose complete control over my life because of one bad case of rotten sushi?

Out of the corner of my eye I see Curtis escorting Jas in the door like some sort of afterthought, with Tessa in tow. I cringe when Jas's eyes meet mine. She looks confused. I shrug my shoulders to communicate that I didn't know what was going on.

"Jasmine." Chase says her name in a sweet whisper and gives her a hug. "Feeling better? You look great!"

Did he hug her longer than he hugged me? *Stop it!*

Tessa grabs Chase's hand. "Hi! I'm Tessa! I'm totally your biggest fan!"

Mom's eyes narrow slightly, but I'm probably the only one who notices. Tessa surely wouldn't. She gives new meaning to the word clueless.

Chase is nothing but courteous and invites Tessa

to the concert, too. This could be my lucky break. Tessa can take my place, and I won't even need to go. Maybe I can get out of going tonight as well.

I look at Chase and wonder if I really *want* to get out of it.

What if…?

No. I have to remember… he and I are impossible.

~~~

Of course, I don't get out of it. A few hours later, we're sitting at a semi-private table in the back of *Ciao*. Tessa is dancing with Chase. Apparently, *she's* not concerned that Jas has staked her claim on him. His bodyguards follow him wherever he goes, even on the dance floor. They remind me of the Secret Service. Strangers keep bothering him, and by the look on his face, I think maybe he wishes he wasn't here either.

Jas is talking to Nick, the drummer in Chase's band, while I pretend to be listening to the music, which I am *not*. The music is terrible. I know not everyone's into Country Pop music like I am, but really, this techno garbage they're playing makes no sense at all.

At least I've finally pulled myself together. I'll just get through tonight, make up some excuse about the concert, and *voila!* I won't see Chase again until the next perfume ad. No problem.

When Chase finally pries himself away from Tessa, he comes back to the table and stands there all adorable looking. Can't he just go away?

"Would you like to dance?" he asks *me*.

Oh, blazes! He looks cuter than a speckled pup. "I don't dance," I shout over the noise. "And besides, I hate this kind of music."

"Me, too!" he shouts back. He whispers something to one of his bodyguards, a huge guy with a really kind baby face. A total contradiction. The bodyguard talks to a nearby waitress. The next thing I know the club manager comes to the table.

"Want to go somewhere quiet so we can talk?" Chase speaks directly into my ear, and then looks at me with that infuriating, puppy-dog look.

I'm thinking I'm not buying it. I'm thinking *no* as I'm nodding my head *yes*. What am I doing?

Chase shouts to the group, "We'll be right back." I see Jasmine and Tessa look at us quizzically. Jas raises her eyebrows at me. I shrug.

The club manager escorts Chase and me, along with the Big Guy, to what must be the manager's own private lounge. He leaves us there, while Big Guy stands outside the door. As soon as it closes behind us, I'm startled by how quiet it is. The same music from the club is piped in at an almost imperceptible volume from speakers on the ceiling. There's a table, some chairs, and a sofa. The room is dark and reminds me of some scene from a mob movie. I shudder.

"We couldn't talk out there," Chase says. "I couldn't hear you well enough."

"Well, this room is kind of creepy. Is this where you like to bring unsuspecting girls?" I try to sound angry.

"No! I've never been here before." Chase frowns and his eyebrows scrunch up. He looks at me earnestly. "It's because...we couldn't go outside. I can't just walk down the street like everyone else."

"So you just whisk girls off into creepy dark lairs instead?"

"You're right. Let's go back." He looks like he really does feel bad, but then he says, "Can we just sit down for a minute?"

I don't answer, but plop down on one of the chairs. I know I'm crossing the line with Jas, but the truth is, the quiet and solitude in here is such a relief. I'm not looking forward to returning to techno-land any time soon.

"So...your sister says you still live in Texas." Chase sits on the couch across from me.

"Yeah." I don't elaborate.

"Me, too. When we're not touring, anyway." Silence. Chase fidgets. Is he nervous? "It's nice to hang out with a fellow Texan."

"Mmmm." I'm not trying to be rude; I've just never been good at making small talk. I try to think of something to say.

Chase looks at me intently. "What kind of music do you like?"

"Actually, I prefer country—but cool country."

"Me, too," Chase says. "I like a lot of different music—except for this stuff they play here." He laughs softly.

Should I have mentioned his music as well? Jas plays it almost non-stop, blaring it from her bedroom at all hours of the day. It's pop, not country, but I do like it, even though it gets a little annoying after you hear someone play the same song ten times in a row.

"Are you coming to the concert tomorrow night?" Chase looks at me. His eyes are soft and serious. Do I hear a little insecurity in his voice?

"About that..." I try to think of an excuse that doesn't sound too lame. "Um... I...I don't think I can." I stand up. "We better get back."

Chase stands, too, and walks over to me. Suddenly he doesn't seem so insecure. "Why don't you like me, Lily? Have I done something wrong?" He touches me and my whole arm tingles. I suck in my breath.

I get this overwhelming urge to reach up and kiss him. I shake my head a little to get my senses back. "What part of 'I have a boyfriend' don't you understand?" I say, without conviction. I breathe deep, frozen in place.

"This part." He bends down and kisses me softly on the mouth.

I stand there and let him kiss me. I can't help it. The only restraint I manage is that I don't really kiss him back.

There's a knock on the door.

"I'm sorry," Chase whispers. "I shouldn't have

done that." He takes a step back.

"Not like it's the first time," I quip, trying to make light of it. My hands are shaking. I move away from him as the door opens.

"Excuse me, Mr. Donovan..." Chase's bodyguard holds the door open as Jas brushes past him into the room.

"There you are!" Jas smiles brightly. "Lily, it's after midnight, and you are *fifteen*...I told Mom we'd be home by one."

I know it's a lie. As long as we're with Chase Donovan, Mom couldn't care less if we didn't come home for a week. I'm so embarrassed I can't speak.

Jas acts as if it's perfectly normal that Chase and I are alone in this room and goes on chattering in her perkiest voice. "I can't wait for the concert tomorrow night! What time should we arrive at the Garden?"

~~~

Luckily, Tessa is spending the night, and Jas doesn't say a word to me about Chase on the way home. Strangely, neither does Tessa. Tessa goes on and on about the drummer, Nick. I lean back on the seat in the town car and pretend to be falling asleep. I can almost feel Chase's lips on mine as I relive the kiss over and over. When Dylan kissed me, it actually felt kind of gross.

I feel a giant pile of guilt about Jas, and another huge pile about Dylan. He promised he would wait for me to come back, that he wouldn't date any other girls while I was away. I didn't promise the same. I didn't have to. It didn't cross my mind that I would meet a boy while I was here. That I would fall like a bale of hay from the barn loft.

Seven

"When one lives in the medium of the roses, one takes in spite of oneself the perfume of it." ~Russian proverb

A limo comes to pick us up at four in the afternoon. The concert doesn't start till seven, but it will take awhile to get there. And Chase promised us a backstage experience that Jas and Tessa wouldn't miss for all the designer shoes in the world. Jas started getting ready at noon. Really. She did. How can such a naturally pretty girl take four whole hours to beautify?

I sit across from Tessa and Jas in the limo, facing the back window, wondering what Jas is really thinking. Early this morning, a ton of designer clothes arrived at our building—for me—in my size—all complimentary. Mom was thrilled. Designers from all over sent me freebies now that I'm the new *Royale Princesse* girl—and

Chase Donovan's new fling. Mom has never treated me so well on one hand, and so smugly on the other. She's practically swimming in "I-told-you-so," her perfume *du jour*.

Jasmine was giddy over my new clothes, looking to see if there was anything she could snag for herself. "You can have anything you want," I said as Jas rifled through them. "I don't care."

"Girls." Mom put her hand up in her *everybody-halt* position. "These designers have given these clothes exclusively to Lily. Jasmine, you know why. So *Lily* will be seen wearing them. Not her sister. Back off."

Jasmine looked stunned, hurt really. I gave her a sympathetic look and mouthed the word *later*. How did the tables turn so quickly? Jas has always been Mom's favorite. She gave up on me long ago—I was nobody to her— and she was nobody to me. And that was the way I liked it.

I lean my head back against the seat in the limo and close my eyes, trying to ignore Tessa's chatter and not think about the other delivery we had this morning. Three giant bouquets from Dad. One for Jas because she'd been sick, one for Mom to congratulate her on the launch of her new perfume, and one for me. Mine was two dozen yellow roses encircled by a row of white lilies. Daddy knows that yellow roses are my favorite. Not only because they're a symbol of Texas, but because they remind me of sunshine. I mean, who can stay blue with a yellow rose around? The note said, "Congratulations, sweetheart. I miss you."

When I read the note, I swallowed hard and squeezed my eyelids shut so I wouldn't cry. Mom said he left a message for me to call him, but I don't know what to say. *I've fallen into their trap? I'm still your little country girl?*

I finger the silver sequins on my new, skin-tight, white jeans. Mom chose my outfit for me, including this flowing, silvery top, and of course, heels. At least this time they're chunky and easier to walk in. They're made of light gray snakeskin and remind me of Texas—a little—even though they don't look like rattler.

Mom's personal hairdresser came and straightened my hair, extensions included, to a long, swingy sheen, and Gaston came again with Samantha to do our make-up. I mean really, doesn't he have a life? I grab a piece of my hair and examine it. It's amazing how hard it is to tell what part is mine and what's not.

"You owe your sister, big time, after what happened last night." Tessa's icy voice startles me back to reality. She takes a sip of the sparkling pear juice she's poured into a champagne glass, and bites into a chocolate covered strawberry, all compliments of Chase.

"What are you talking about?" I look out the window and away from her stare.

"You know, going off with Chase like that when you know your sister likes him." She looks at me like I'm a total moron.

"Leave her alone," Jas says before I can answer.

I'm glad, because I don't know *how* to answer. I

should have said no when he asked me to go somewhere quiet. I have no excuse.

Jas takes the platter out of Tessa's hand. "Stop eating those strawberries. You're ruining your lipstick, and you've got chocolate on your teeth." Jas pulls out a compact. "Here, fix yourself."

That's another one of Mom's rules. Resist food, especially before an event. You don't want to spill on your clothes, ruin your make-up, or—*Mom* forbid—have a puffy stomach. And when you're being followed by paparazzi, you don't want to risk a shot of you stuffing your face ending up in a gossip rag.

Tessa takes the compact and cleans her teeth with a tissue, then reapplies her lip-gloss. She makes a smacking sound and clamps the compact shut. "I'm just saying, there's a code of honor, you know, between sisters." She hands Jas back the compact. "And best friends."

"She knows," Jas says smiling at me. Maybe she's not mad after all. And I will make it very clear to Chase today that I'm not interested. Period. I can do this. Even if it's a lie.

When we get to the Garden, I can't believe the mass of young girls everywhere, most of them holding up glittery homemade signs and wearing T-shirts with Chase's face plastered on them. Some girls scream and chase our limo. I guess it's because the windows are dark and they can't tell who's inside. I don't see anyone our age. Only younger kids and their mothers, and even a dad or two.

Getting from the limo to the door is total chaos. Cameras flash, and girls scream. People are pushing and shoving. It takes about five body guards to escort us in. Tessa is laughing hysterically. Jas is perfectly poised. Once the door shuts behind us, I feel relieved. I don't know how Chase can stand to live like this.

As soon as I see him, my heart jumps and then pounds. He's wearing white jeans, too, and an un-tucked, blue dress shirt the same color as his eyes. He gives each one of us a hug and a kiss on the cheek. He kisses me last, and it lands a little low on the back of my jaw. I feel his breath for a brief second in my ear. He smells like peppermint... and soap... and... and a little of *Royale* for men.

Our eyes meet. His are smiling. I look away first.

Jas's phone bleeps. She looks down at it and quickly stops the incoming call. She and Tessa exchange glances. A woman comes over and hands us each a lanyard with a VIP tag attached. Jas and Tessa put theirs on, but I just hold mine. Jas gives me a look.

"What?" I whisper. She raises her eyebrows at me, so I loop it over my head and pull my hair—well it's not really *my* hair—up and over it.

We follow Chase to his dressing room. "You guys can hang out here or wander around if you like. I have a few things to take care of before the concert." He grabs a ruby red guitar that's leaning against the wall. "Help yourselves to anything you want." He looks at me and smiles before closing the door.

The first thing Tessa does is run to the food table.

"Tessa, no!" Jas yells. "Stay away from the snacks. Haven't I taught you anything?"

Tessa ignores her and samples a piece of cheese.

I join Tessa at the table. "I don't care about Mom's rule, I'm hungry. I'll just have something small and not messy." I scan the choices. Fruit… cheese… gummy bears? No, they stick to your teeth. "Beef jerky! Perfect!" It's not your ordinary beef jerky, but big, Texas style jerky. I guess Chase *is* a true Texan after all. I put a huge piece in my mouth and tug.

"Ugh!" Tessa wrinkles her nose. "You're going to smell like meat. Or dead horses."

"She's right," Jas says. "Hey, look at this." She picks up framed picture of a pretty girl. A very pretty girl.

"She's gorgeous." Tessa takes the photo out of Jas's hand. "I knew he had a girlfriend, and I knew it wasn't that skank, Bibi Johnson."

Jas told me there were rumors about him and Bibi, ever since he made a guest appearance on her show. "How do you know that's his girlfriend?" I say, with a mouthful of jerky. "Let me see."

As soon as I grab the frame the door opens. It's Chase. I'm standing there holding his supposed girlfriend's picture with a big hunk of jerky hanging out of my mouth. Perfect.

"That's my sister." Chase strides in the room. "I forgot something." He winks at me and grabs a little piece of plastic off the dressing table. "My lucky pick."

The door closes and Tessa and Jas break out laughing. Hysterically. I set the picture down on the dressing table, dying of embarrassment. I spit the jerky out in the waste basket just as Chase pops his head back in.

"Glad you're enjoying yourselves!" He looks right at me—in mid-spit—and closes the door again.

Could this get any worse? I look at Jas and Tessa. For a second I think I'm going to cry, but then I burst out laughing. We laugh so hard our eyes water and all three of us have to fix our make-up. So much for making a good impression. If Mom knew that Chase saw me spit beef jerky out of my mouth, she'd faint, for real. It never fails. Mom's rules always prove to be helpful in the end. Why can't I learn to follow them?

Before the concert begins, we're led to a hidden area on stage. We sit on squishy folding chairs between two curtains. Chase's mom is with us. She keeps smiling at Jas. Jas smiles back with this sweet, angelic look on her face.

The lights dim. Tessa whoops and hollers until Jas grabs her arm. Can't she show a little restraint? The show hasn't even started yet. I take a deep breath and fold my hands on my lap. I'm nervous. For Chase. I don't know how he can perform in front of all these people.

After the warm-up band finishes—a girl band that has me suddenly feeling jealous—I look around for Chase. I haven't seen him since I spit the jerky in his waste basket. His entire band is now on stage, except him, and the crowd is screeching.

The stage begins to fill with bright blue fog. A trap door opens in the middle of the floor, and Chase slowly rises into the smoke, only visible as a silhouette.

Excitement vibrates through the air, making the hair on my arms stand up. I feel my heart pounding in my ears, despite the screams from the audience that are almost deafening. Why do I feel this way? I do *not* want to be here. I do *not* want to like this. I do not want to like *him*. This is all silly nonsense. Proof that Chase is some phony star. I close my eyes and pretend I'm riding Fire Star. I won't let Chase get to me.

Tessa jabs me in the ribs and I glare at her. I'd tell her where to go, but there's no way she'd hear me. I exhale. I'll just enjoy the music. That's all.

Chase must be singing every song he's ever recorded. Some I've never even heard before. When he gets to our song—I mean the one he sang to me in the commercial—I catch my breath. He's changed into a gray hoodie with dark jeans, and he's sitting on a stool, playing his guitar. I close my eyes and pretend he's singing only to me.

Tessa jabs me again, and I open my eyes. I'm about to smack her hand, until I see Chase walking across the stage—still singing with his head-piece—his guitar hanging across his shoulder. Coming straight toward me. *Everyone*—his mom, his stage manager, Jasmine, me—is looking at him like he's lost his mind. He waves for me to come to him, and when I don't, he jogs the rest of the way and drags me onto the stage.

Fear seizes me, but I allow him to lead me to the stool, where he sits me down, takes both of my hands in his, and sings to me. The crowd is in an uproar. I can't bear to look at him, but know I'll look silly in front of thousands of people if I don't. I glance at his face and finally meet his gaze. It's so intense, like it's only him and me in this room—this stadium—and not a gazillion other people. A gazillion girls that love him.

He squeezes my hand right before he lets go on the last note. As a blue mist envelops us, two crew members dressed in black escort me back to my seat. The band is already starting a new song when I hear Chase yell out on his microphone, "Lets here it for Lily, everybody!"

Jas is grimacing, Mrs. Donovan looks confused, and Tessa's mouth is hanging open. I run past them backstage, shaking like the drummer's tambourine.

Was this for publicity, or could he really like me? But if I like him back... and this is all for show? The thought stabs at my heart. It would be embarrassing. Devastating. I wipe away a tear that catches me by surprise.

Eight

"We live with our defects as with the odors which we carry; we do not smell them anymore; they inconvenience only the others." ~Anne Thérèse de Marguenat de Courcelles

When I come down for breakfast the next morning, Mom's in the formal dining room with an elegantly dressed woman, the entire table covered in party theme samples. There are scrapbooks, display boards, and extravagant party favors spread from one end to the other. I take a detour to the kitchen, hoping they won't see me, but Mom looks up just as I try to scurry out of sight.

"Lily! Please come," she calls. I feel like a puppy in obedience school.

"Here's the birthday girl," she singsongs when I appear, casting a frown my way as her eyes take note of my pajamas. "Lily, this is Maxine Silver. I've hired her to plan your Sweet Sixteen. Max, this is Lily."

I nod and say hello. I realize I've been elevated to something akin to royalty by just this simple address, despite Mom's condescending tone when she speaks to me. Mom never, and I mean *never*, breaches etiquette. And since Ms. Silver is at least thirty years older than I am, and Mom introduced *her* to me first, that speaks volumes.

My mind plays the script titled, Hya's Rules of Etiquette. *When making introductions, always address the person of highest stature first. Age is always the determining factor, unless there are clear and obvious distinctions in social hierarchy.* I'm a living archive of my mother's rules. It takes a minute for the words "Sweet Sixteen" to sink in.

"Mother..." I smile through clenched teeth. "Remember, I'm not having a Sweet Sixteen party here in New York. We agreed I'd spend my birthday with Dad, in *Texas.*"

"Things have changed." Mom's smile is laced with warning. "I've already called and invited your father."

I know Mom, and I can see the wheels turning as she decides to dismiss me. "Lily is much too busy to concern herself with these details." She turns to me. "Run along now, darling. Maxine is the best party planner in the city. Even with such short notice, your party will be fabulous." She gestures me to leave with a sweep of her hand. "Not to worry!"

I narrow my eyes at Mom. She can't do this to me. We had a deal. I would spend the whole summer in New York, but be allowed one weekend—my birthday weekend—in Texas. I bite my tongue and storm into the kitchen. Jas is at the breakfast table, nibbling on some cantaloupe from a tiny fruit plate with a miniscule serving of bran cereal next to it.

I pull a bowl from the cupboard and slam it down on the table.

"Ouch. What's wrong with you?"

"*Mom* is what's wrong with me! I don't know why you chose to live with her! She's…evil!" I grab the cereal box and shake it over my bowl until it spills over.

Jas throws her head back and laughs. "Evil? You're funny."

"This is so not funny! She doesn't care what I want. Two more years. Two more years and that's it! I will never have to spend another minute with her again as long as I live!"

"Harsh. She just wants what's best for us." Jas takes a bite of cereal. "You're so ungrateful."

I dump half of the cereal back in the box and pour the milk, splashing it outside the bowl. "You like this life. I don't. Why can't you and Mom get that?"

"You're a spoiled brat," Jas says.

"*I'm* a spoiled brat?"

"Yeah, you." Jas gets up and puts her dishes in the sink and then turns to face me. "Mom can be difficult, true, but just deal with it already. And one thing's for sure, she didn't raise us to whine and complain."

"Raise *us*? She abandoned me."

"That was your choice."

"Hmm… let's see. Leave Daddy and everything I love behind for this? Easy choice."

Jas walks out the door without another word. I dump my cereal into the sink, no longer hungry. I can't believe Little Miss High Society called *me* a brat. When Mom decided her career was more important than our family, Jas chose this lifestyle over Dad and me. Plain and simple.

An hour later Mom calls a "family" meeting. Curtis and Ingrid are included, supposedly so they're aware of our schedules. Mom's lucky they're here to keep me civil. I'm so mad about my birthday I might just stand up to her once and for all. She has us sit around the huge mahogany dining room table, now cleared of all party paraphernalia, like it's her boardroom. I sit down with a can of soda, being careful to use a coaster. I know Mom hates when I drink out of a can, but it tastes better to me that way.

"Ingrid," Mom says, pointing to my drink. "Please replace that with a *diet* soda." Ingrid grabs the can and scurries to the kitchen while my mouth drops open.

Mom stands at the foot of the table, clearly in command, and doesn't even look at me. She waits for Ingrid to return with my diet soda, this time in a glass, wrapped in a napkin, with a straw. "By the way, Lily," Mom says to me. "W*ater* is a model's best friend." I roll my eyes.

Mom clears her throat, in a lady-like way of course. "There will be a Sweet Sixteen party for Lily in three weeks. At the Plaza. The theme will be Cinderella."

I'm in the middle of sipping my drink. I choke, and soda spurts from the top of my straw. "Excuse me? Isn't that a little juvenile?"

"Not Disney's Cinderella, Lily. Think Rodgers and Hammerstein's." Mom looks at me like I'm an idiot. "It will be perfect."

I want to say, *does that make you and Jas like evil "steps?"* but think better of it. Even though they're not my stepfamily, it sure feels like it sometimes. And why is it always the evil "stepmother" anyway? Is there some bias against evil real mothers?

"How about a Hans Christian Anderson's *Ugly Duckling* theme while you're at it?" I blurt out. That one I couldn't resist.

"Hmm, that would mean you're admitting I've turned you into a swan," Mom says without the hint of a smile. She always wins.

"The ballroom at the Plaza was recently renovated, entirely in antique white and gold. It's very Old World European, the perfect backdrop," Mom continues. She looks directly at me. "You are very lucky that Ms. Silverman was able to secure it at such short notice."

That's me! Lucky, lucky me!

"On Friday we are leaving for Paris to prepare for

the next perfume shoot," Mom states matter-of-factly. "In the meantime, we have a lot to do. Lily, we must plan your wardrobe for Paris. We have an appointment at Francesca's in an hour. Please be ready promptly."

Why do I still feel like I'm on some horrific amusement park ride? I should have jumped out of the limousine the minute Jas started barfing.

The Queen dismisses us. I don't bother trying again to convince her to drop the Sweet Sixteen party. Once Mom has launched a battleship, my measly little weapons are like suction cup darts bouncing off the Titanic. An iceberg sunk the Titanic, true, but I already know Mom is immune to ice. Three cold years are proof of that. The Ice Queen isn't affected by anyone's cold shoulder, and she doesn't deserve any warmth. She'd only take advantage of it.

I shower, put my hair in a ponytail and go back downstairs, sans make-up. I wonder how Dad feels about me not coming home for my birthday. I need to talk to Dylan, too, but I don't know what to say. Should I break up with him for real? At least the fact that I'm not going back to Texas any time soon gives me more time.

Mom is nowhere to be seen, so I tell Ingrid to let Mom know I'll be waiting for her in the lobby. That way she won't comment on my attire and make me go change. I take the elevator down and pick a puffy wing chair to sink into. It's quiet. Everyone here goes away this time of year—the Hamptons, Maine, somewhere cool—but not Mom. She's all about work. The only vacation she takes is a few days at Meme's villa near Paris. But even there, it's all about business.

Mom has replaced my Indian tote bag with a giant Louis Vuitton, big enough to carry a litter of puppies in. I pull out *Jane Eyre* and start to read.

Jane Eyre is my favorite book of all time. Mostly because I love Jane's courage and the banter between her and Mr. Rochester. And maybe because I imagine Mom to be as cruel as Jane's benefactor, Mrs. Reed. I've got Dad, so I can't consider myself an orphan, but when your Mom takes up and leaves when you're only twelve years old, it can feel that way sometimes.

It's true, I could have gone with her, but I would have had to leave behind Dad and the ranch and Texas—all the things I love more than anything in the world. How can a mother ask her child to do that?

I've read only a few pages when I hear a man's voice tell George he has a package for Lily Laroche Carter. Maybe an early birthday present? I stash my book back into my bag and go to the foyer.

"Ah, Mademoiselle Lily," George says. "We have a package for you." He likes to address Mom, Jas, and me in French. He thinks it impresses Mom, and since he's always so sweet to me, I play along.

"Merci Beaucoup, George." I give him a big smile and take the small box, wrapped in plain brown packing paper. It's addressed to me, with no sign of who it's from. Dylan maybe? I take it back to my chair and rip off the paper, finding a bag of 100% pure Texas Beef Jerky and a hand-written note inside.

> *Lily,*
>
> *Sorry I couldn't see you after the concert last night. I'm leaving tomorrow. Can I see you today? I thought we could sneak away, incognito, and see a bit of the city.*
>
> *Please call me.*

It's signed Chase, with a cell phone number scribbled at the bottom. I cringe at the memory of Chase seeing me spit in his dressing room, but I laugh out loud. Sending me beef jerky is funny, and so sweet. What now? Do I want to see him? I shouldn't... but...

Should I call him? Believe it or not, I have never ever called a boy—except for Dylan the other day in Jasmine's closet—and that was an emergency. Even though I don't live with Mom full time anymore, there has never been a firmer rule, one that even I don't break: *Do not call boys. Boys must call you. Period. No exceptions.* But Chase asked me to call him, and he couldn't call me, at least not on a cell, since I don't have one. And not at the apartment, if he wanted to see me in secret. That brings up another rule: *If a boy wants to see you in secret, if he ever wants to hide something—the answer is a firm no.*

But Chase and I have a reason to hide. More than one. For him, at least the paparazzi. And maybe that girl in the picture. For me, the paparazzi, Dylan, Jasmine. Plus, I don't want to give Mom the satisfaction. And it's possible she might still want Jasmine to have her chance with Chase—though I doubt that.

Mom *would* find it incredibly rude if I didn't thank him for the gift. I go to George and ask if I can use his cell phone.

"Why not use the desk phone, my cherub?"

"Um… it's a delicate situation."

"Of course, Mademoiselle." George takes a small black cell phone out of his doorman's coat. He turns it on, explaining to me that he can't use it when he's working.

"Any restrictions?" I ask. "This is long distance. I'll pay you."

"Continental USA?"

"Tokyo," I tease. "Just kidding. Yes."

"Won't cost me a dime. It's all yours."

"Thanks, George!" I take the phone and walk a few feet away, standing clear of the doorway. I can see a couple of cameramen hanging around outside the building and realize they're probably there for me.

I call Chase, and when he answers, I don't use his name, in case anyone in the lobby is listening.

"Hi, it's Lily. Thanks for the jerky."

"Hey!" Pause. "Did you enjoy the concert last night?"

"I have a few choice words for you for bringing me on stage like that! Could you prepare a girl a little?"

"Sorry! It was an impulse. Every time I looked over at you…"

Silence.

"Sorry," Chase finally whispers.

"No, it's okay. It was really sweet."

"Can I see you today?"

"My mother's taking me shopping. Maybe when I get back? But it won't be easy for me to call you. I don't have a cell phone right now."

"Why not?" Chase asks.

"Long story." I can't tell him the real reason—that my parents are trying to keep me away from a boy. "How's two o'clock? We could meet somewhere?"

"Perfect. I'd pick you up, but the paparazzi would tail us for sure. Can you sneak out of your building and meet me somewhere close by?"

We decide to meet at the New York Public Library on Fifth Avenue. Rose Reading Room. Two o'clock. I'm about to say goodbye when an arm reaches over me and snatches George's cell phone out of my hand.

"Who is this?" Mom speaks into the phone, her eyes flashing. When no one answers, she turns to me. "Where did you get this?"

I stand there speechless, not wanting to get George in trouble.

"It's my phone, Madame Laroche. Is everything okay?" George stands in front of Mom like a soldier at attention.

"Everything is fine, George. Thank you." Mom smiles at George sweetly and hands him the phone. I relax, realizing Mom would never admit to banning me from the telephone in public. And even though I've seen her berate George a time or two, she's generally polite to him, always conscious of her image.

"George, I wouldn't like to see you lose your job over Lily's inconsiderate request. You know that doormen at the Triumph are not allowed to be seen using cell phones while on duty. Please refrain in the future."

"Yes, Madame. I apologize."

"It's quite all right. Come along now, Lily. Curtis is waiting with the car out front."

"There are paparazzi, Madame."

"I am aware." Mom smiles at George serenely. "Thank you."

As soon as George opens the door of our building, cameras start flashing. "Where ya off to, Lily?" A man with a huge camera shouts. Mom firmly guides me toward the town car. "Lily, over here!" another one yells. We keep moving.

I give George a sympathetic look as he opens the car door. He pats my arm as I climb in, and then shuts the door behind me. I wave at him through the window.

"For heaven's sake, Lily, do not wave at doormen," Mom chides.

I sit back against the black leather seat and wait for the inquisition to begin.

"I assume you were talking to that juvenile delinquent of yours. Don't try to deny it." Surprisingly, Mom sounds calm. "He's no good for you, Lily. You must forget him."

"Why? Because he's a ranch hand? He's trying to

make it in the music industry—like Chase Donovan. Isn't that good enough?"

Mom snorts. "Believe it or not, this is not about his social status—although I've told you many times that things never work out between people of two drastically different worlds. Your father says he's trouble, and I trust his judgment. A boy like that is only out for what he can get from you. Open your eyes."

"Did it occur to you that maybe he likes me—for me?" *Unlike you* I add silently.

"My, but you're naive. You always have lived in that little imaginary world of yours. People are out for themselves. The sooner you learn that, the better off you'll be."

If Mom is referring to herself, I have to agree with her. She *is* out only for herself. I almost say so but decide better of it. I don't bother telling Mom that it wasn't even Dylan I was talking to. What's the point? If I tell her about Chase, she'll either be glad about it and stick herself in the middle to control it, or destroy it so her favorite daughter's dream isn't crushed. I think it's probably the first one. I don't think she'd care about Jas's little crush if she thought either one of her daughters had half a chance with Chase Donovan.

The last thing I want is for Hya Laroche to be in control of my love life. Besides, Chase is a pop star. Let's be realistic. Not exactly boyfriend material if you ask me. More like a heartache waiting to happen. I start to doubt whether meeting him today is such a good idea after all.

Mom hands me her cell phone. "Here's someone you *should* talk to—your father. When I told him about your birthday this morning, he said you never returned his call."

She's already dialed his number. I hate when she does that. It's ringing. I'm not prepared. I haven't talked to him since before the commercial, and I still don't know what to say.

"Daddy?" I'm all choked up.

"Lily! You're sure hard to get a hold of. How's my girl?"

"Fine." *Am I?* "I miss you."

"I miss you too. Now tell me how my little cowgirl ended up in a big commercial?" His voice is light, supportive even, but of course it would be. Even if it bothered him, he'd never let it show. My eyes tear up at the thought of how good he is to me.

"Well, Jas was sick and they needed someone, like, right then, and I was just standing there and...." I take a deep breath. "Then, poof! I'm in a commercial!"

"Well, you sure looked pretty."

"Thanks, Dad." I change the subject. "How's Fire Star?"

"She's fine. She's had quite a few of those little apples you told me to give her." He chuckles.

"Give her a hug for me. And one for you too, Dad." I close my eyes. "I love you."

"I love you, too, Lilykins. See you on your birthday."

I hang up the phone. Of course he's not *mad*—he almost never is. The closest to mad I've ever seen him was when Dylan and I skipped school, but it was mostly directed at Dylan, not me. But there was something far worse than anger in his eyes that day. Disappointment. The look on his face was worse than any punishment could ever be.

I hand Mom back her phone. She's got this indescribable look on her face. I can't tell if it's annoyance, or maybe just ambivalence, but it's definitely not sympathy. She launches in about how much work there is to do on my wardrobe before we leave for Paris.

As soon as we enter Francesca's, at least five people lavish attention on us. It kind of makes me feel like a princess, but it's uncomfortable—and weird. First they measure me in my bra and underwear, which is totally embarrassing, and then I sit on a comfy sofa in a soft white robe while Mom lets everyone know her expectations for my wardrobe. A young woman offers us food and something to drink, but Mom only allows me to have chilled water with a slice of lemon.

Why are we even here? Why aren't the freebies that were sent to me enough for her? I try on outfit after outfit, standing on a large, carpeted platform in front of a huge three-way mirror. The Queen makes her declarations: yes or no. She's very decisive—taking only seconds for each ensemble. A few times I try to voice my opinion, but I'm completely ignored. If it's a yes, three or four people start pinning and poking. Another brings accessories that Mom herself whips up on me, shouting out ideas for more as someone else scurries to find what she's looking for. If they don't have it, they take notes to get it.

My face is flushed and I can feel little drops of perspiration on my forehead. I've been putting garments on and off for at least an hour, pinned here and pinned there. Enough already. When I think I can't take another minute, it's over.

Mom has chosen at least three evening gowns for me, but she didn't say which one would be for my party. I go up and touch a light blue silk Versace, imagining it must be the one.

"Is this what I'm wearing to my Sweet Sixteen?" I ask.

"No, that's for a photo shoot. Your Sweet Sixteen's a costume party. Your ball gown is already being designed and made in Paris. I took care of that this morning. You'll go for a fitting while we're there."

Ball gown? Isn't that a little over the top? And Mom thinks *I* live in my own little world? I imagine the ridiculously overdone affair that my Sweet Sixteen party is destined to be. I know what Mom is like. I cringe when I remember Jas's Sweet Sixteen, an extravagant Arabian Night's themed party that included live camel rides and a belly-dancing harem. People are still talking about it almost two years later.

I sigh, realizing I have no choice. Mom will do it her way, no matter what. Thank goodness I'm only here till the end of the summer, and then this nightmare will be over. There's only one week left in June, and then the whole month of July—bleh—but only half of August. After that, I'll be back in Texas, galloping through the fields on Fire Star. Blissfully *alone*.

Just. Get. Through.

But what about Chase? When summer's over, will he be over, too?

Mom talks business on her cell phone all the way back to the apartment, giving me time to think up a plan. I need to get to the library by two, without Mom or Jas, or—I just remember—the paparazzi, knowing where I am going. But hey, it is the library, and Mom knows I'm a bookworm. She often ridicules it, after all. And Jas wouldn't be surprised—or want to join me—so maybe the truth would work. Except for the pap. But I think I have an idea for them, too.

I wait until we're in the elevator and Mom tells me she has to go to her empire, a.k.a., the office. "Mom, is it okay if I go to the library today?"

She rolls her eyes. "Finished reading the complete works of Shakespeare already?"

"Actually, they lied. A few of his works were missing."

Mom rolls her eyes again. "Curtis can take you when he brings me to the office." She steps out of the elevator that leads directly into our apartment. "We're leaving in five."

I rush to my room to get a few things. Mom would

think it's odd if I change to go to the library, but Chase has never seen me without designer clothes and tons of make-up. I grab a cute top out of the bag of ready-mades that Mom bought me today and roll it up small, tucking it inside my giant Louis.

When Mom and I walked into the apartment, I heard Jas and Tessa laughing in the den, so I decide it's safe to help myself to some of Jas's make-up. Until the perfume commercial, I'd made a point of barely wearing any to spite Mom, but I'm not sure Chase would even recognize me if I didn't wear a least some. Piles of it line the vanity in Jas's bathroom. I grab a little of everything. Eyeliner, mascara, a pink pot of something that should double as a lipstick and blush. She'll never miss it. All I need now is a disguise. I borrow a pair of Dolce and Gabbana sunglasses from Jas's huge collection and grab my own Texas Rangers baseball cap.

Mom's voice calls from the intercom in my room. "Lily, we're leaving."

I stick my copy of Shakespeare on top of all the things in my tote so it looks like I'm only carrying books, and go downstairs. Off to the library! I've never been to a library in New York before, as much as I love libraries. Before I leave Texas to come here every summer, I pack my suitcase full of books. No matter how annoying Mom's world, or where she drags me, they've always been my escape. And up until this summer, it always worked. It was easy for everyone to ignore the little bookworm sister.

In the car I tell Mom and Curtis I don't want the pap following me, so to throw them off, I'm going to hide on the seat after Mom is dropped off in the parking garage. They won't bother following Curtis in an empty car. Mom thinks it's an excellent idea, not thrilled with my attire, nor the idea of paparazzi following me to a library. She says something along the lines of it's time to shed my bookworm identity and emerge from my cocoon as the butterfly that I am. Blah. Blah. Blah.

My plan works perfectly. Curtis drops me off in front of the library fifteen minutes ahead of schedule, and there isn't a camera in sight. I practically skip through the doors I'm so proud of myself.

I stop dead in my tracks as soon as I take in the beauty of the library. Libraries always make my heart pound, sort of like Chase does. All the possibilities stacked in all those books. But I've never seen a library like this one. I take a deep breath. I totally forget why I'm here and attempt to get a library card. The only identification I have is a Texas State learner's permit—a no go. I ask a librarian where I can find the Rose Reading Room and a bathroom, and he gives me directions to both. Third floor.

I take the stairs. I know I should go straight to the bathroom, but I can't help myself from walking into the reading room first. I stand there with my mouth open, staring up at the painted ceiling. It's so beautiful—a cloudy blue sky—nearly as pretty as the sky in Texas.

I search the large room for a glimpse of Chase. My

heart stops. I see him standing at the end of a table, thumbing through a reference book on a pedestal. He's wearing a knit skater cap and glasses, not sunglasses, but real glasses. I wonder if he needs them or if they're just part of his disguise. It took me a minute to realize it was him, so I guess his disguise is working. After all, I'm the only one in this library expecting to see Chase Donovan. I tip-toe away to find the bathroom.

Minutes later I emerge, slightly better dressed, but still me. My new top. Blue Jeans. Converse. My cowboy boots never did reappear, and I haven't had a chance to find new ones. I'm not wearing even half the make-up Chase is used to seeing me in, but who cares? Let's see if Chase even recognizes me without a Gaston job.

My confidence disappears the minute I see Chase. Should I go back and put on more make-up? Am I pretty enough without it? I stop at the end of a row of tables, unable to move my feet. Should I be wearing my disguise, too? But I've only been... famous is not the right word— for what—three days? No one will recognize *me*. Besides, the clientele at the library hardly look like pop music fans. Not a teeny bopper in sight.

I watch as Chase looks in the opposite direction from where I'm standing, searching for *me*. He's so adorable. Finally, he looks my way. I just stand there at the end of the row, frozen. Our eyes meet. He doesn't smile. Neither do I. Suddenly it all seems so serious. I take a deep breath and wait.

Chase lets the pages of the book drop and

approaches me. Taking both my hands he whispers, "Lily." And then finally, that smile. That melt-my-heart, knock-me-over, smile. "You made it."

Did he think I wouldn't? I look down at my watch. Two-twenty. I must have burned up a lot of time waiting in line to get a library card. Oh well, Mom would be proud. She always tells us, when it comes to boys: *plant doubts. Be hard to get. Boys will like you more.* I look at Chase's face. So sincere. I don't think it's necessary.

"Of course, I did," I say.

"Let's sit down." Chase leads me to some nearby chairs. "Was it hard for you to escape?"

"No, I told my Mom I needed to find some of the lost works of William Shakespeare." I giggle nervously.

"And she believed you?"

I pull out my five-inch-wide paperback copy of The Complete Works. "Yeah, she believed me."

Chase takes the book from my hands, opens it to a random spot, and starts reading out loud. "Eyes, look your last! Arms, take your last embrace!"

Romeo and Juliet. Act five, scene three.

He looks at me. "Do you have to read this for homework?"

Maybe I shouldn't have showed him. I mean, how un-cool can I be? The truth is, when we read *A Midsummer Night's Dream* in lit class last year, I kind of liked it and wanted to see what else Shakespeare wrote. Instead I say, "Yeah, required summer reading."

I look down. "But I like it."

"I'll have to try it sometime." Chase smiles at me.

A couple of people keep giving us dirty looks. For a place so packed with people, it's eerily quiet. Yeah, I know it's a library, but I thought a library in the heart of New York City wouldn't be quiet for some reason. I was wrong. We decide to leave. Chase throws my giant Louis over his shoulder and takes my hand. "What have you got in this thing?" he whispers. I feel weak in the knees by the touch of his hand. Like a current is traveling from him to me.

"My disguise!"

Before we walk out the door, Chase pulls me to the side. "Maybe you better put it on." He smiles. "You look so pretty. People will stare at you for sure."

He still thinks I'm pretty, even without Gaston! I pull out my Texas Rangers baseball cap and the sunglasses I "borrowed" from Jas. "How's this?"

"Cute!" He says. "But *I'd* still recognize you anywhere!"

I reach up and touch the rim of his glasses. "Are these real or fake?"

"Shh," he whispers with a big smile. "They're real."

Chase takes my hand again and we burst out into the sunshine. As soon as we're out the door, we both start laughing. For no reason. We laugh and hold hands, prancing down the sidewalk.

For the first time in my life...
I heart NYC.

Nine

"Love is like a beautiful flower which I may not touch, but whose fragrance makes the garden a place of delight just the same." ~ Helen Keller

We walk hand in hand toward Central Park, taking in all the sights. I tell him how it breaks my heart to see horses in the city pulling carriages with big heavy tourists riding in them. It's *so* not a life for a horse. Chase agrees. I surprise myself at how chatty I am. Chase is so easy to talk to—he *wants* to know my opinions! I feel alive and free for the first time in weeks.

When we get to the park, we sit on the grass under a tree. I'm so happy to touch a tree that doesn't look all little and scraggly, I feel like hugging it. I breathe deeply, it's like we've entered another world. It's not

Texas, but it's not concrete, either. I'd forgotten how much I like the park.

Chase switched his real glasses for sunglasses as we walked down Fifth Avenue, and now he takes them off and looks at me, smiling. Really *seeing* me. He sure smiles a lot. Not like Dylan, who's too cool to smile.

"You must come to the park a lot," he says, "to get away?"

"I was just wondering why I don't. Mom and Jas are all about work—or parties—I guess. Coming to the park is *not* on the agenda." As soon as the words leave my mouth, I wish I hadn't said them. I don't mean to cast Jas in a bad light, and what she said to me this morning comes to mind. *"Mom didn't raise us to whine and complain."* Is that what I do? Couldn't I ask Curtis to bring me here anytime I wanted to? I decide to change the subject. "What's your favorite part of the city?"

"I'm really not here very much, only for special events and concerts. I'm usually in and out. Spend most of my time in hotels, or on the bus. I haven't even been to the Statue of Liberty."

"You're kidding! My mom's from France, so every French friend and relative that came to visit us when we were growing up had to be taken to see the Statue of Liberty. It's a matter of pride—the greatest gift the United States has ever received, you know. Courtesy of the French!" I groan.

"It must've been great, growing up with all of this... and France... and Texas, too."

I don't know how to answer. I bite my bottom lip. "You know how it is," I finally say.

Chase doesn't answer right away, like he has to think about it. "You know I didn't grow up rich, don't you, Lily?" Chase looks pensive. "It's been less than three years since I recorded my first hit song. Everything happened so fast. Sometimes I still wake up and think I'm dreaming."

We sit quietly for a moment.

"I don't mean we were poor or anything," Chase adds. "There just weren't a lot of extras. Like trips."

I shift against the tree. I'm not naïve. I know I have so much more than the average girl, but how do you tell anyone who hasn't experienced it, that it's not all it's cracked up to be? *You don't.* "I wish I could take you to the Statue of Liberty right now." I sit up straight. "But it's too late to catch the last ferry."

I've always thought if I had to visit Lady Liberty even one more time, I'd die. It's like going to the Eiffel tower over and over again with American friends who visit us in Paris. I can't take it anymore. But going anywhere with Chase sounds fun. And after all, the guy should get to see it up close, at least once.

Chase's eyes light up like a little kid's. "Couldn't we find a boat that'll take us into the middle of the harbor—to get a closer look at it?"

I laugh. "Maybe. But we need to hurry." I get up off the ground and reach my hand out to pull him up. "I have to be back to the library by six."

Chase looks down at his watch. "Think we can we do it?"

"We can try!" I can't stop smiling.

Chase grabs my hand and we run back to Fifth to catch a cab. I stand back and wait to see if he needs any help hailing one, since Mom says it's a man's job. Not that she uses cabs anyway. Even with his hat pulled down and his sunglasses on, Chase has no trouble flagging one down. We plop into the backseat laughing.

"Where to?" the cabbie asks.

"I got this," I say to Chase and lean forward. I tell the cabbie where to take us, and then explain to Chase. "Every once in awhile, Mom makes us take a private cruise with out of town guests."

I check inside my bag for my credit card, since I carry very little cash. Mom and Dad gave me my own card when I was fourteen, so I use it for almost everything. They've never questioned my purchases. It's basically just bookstores and Starbucks. And sometimes the local Feed n' Seed to buy something for Fire Star. Jas's bills must be a million times bigger than mine. She blows more in five minutes at Saks than I do in a year. But still, Mom would definitely question my renting a yacht.

I don't need to worry. When we get to the marina, Chase pulls out a huge money clip full of bills and pays the cab driver. He puts it back in his pocket as the cabbie pulls away, and I hope no one else saw it. They'd either rob us, or call the cops if they did. Chase looks kind of embarrassed. It's like three inches thick.

"Rob any banks lately?" I ask.

Chase laughs. "I know it looks bad, but I always use cash when I don't want to be recognized. One swipe of a credit card and someone always calls the paparazzi." He squeezes my hand. "I don't want anything to ruin our day."

We walk toward the docks. Chase says he'd prefer to go in a sailboat, but that would take too long, and our time is running out. If we told people who he was, we'd probably get a ride anywhere, but it turns out being Hya Laroche's daughter, and having Chase's cash, is enough to get a last minute cruise for two on a high powered speed boat. We tell the captain exactly what we have in mind and he speeds off.

The wind whips at our hats, forcing us to remove them. My hair extensions blow straight back behind me, and I hope Chase can't see the roots. I search inside my bag for a ponytail holder but can't find one. The boat bounces on a wave, and I almost fall off the seat. I grab on to Chase, and we burst out laughing.

I twist my hair and tuck it in my shirt. Nestling into Chase, I lean back and take in the view of the Manhattan skyline. It's spectacular, even to me. How did I ever hate it so much?

The captain takes us to a spot with a perfect view of the Statue of Liberty, and shuts off the engine. The boat slowly drifts on the dark water. I don't want to ruin the moment for Chase, so I don't say a word. I try to imagine I'm seeing Lady Liberty up close for the first time, like he is.

She really is magnificent, when you think about it. Her face is strong. Powerful. Almost frightening. I decide she's my new inspiration. Maybe I'm a lot stronger than I thought I was. Maybe I *can* stand up to Mom and take charge of my life. This is a free country. Liberty and Justice for *all*.

And Jas? She'll understand about Chase. Won't she? I mean, you can't just claim who your boyfriend is. He has to agree, doesn't he?

"Wow." Chase grabs my hand again and looks into my eyes. "She's even more beautiful close up." He raises one eyebrow, like he means me, too, and then laughs. "Thanks for doing this," he says quietly, then turns again toward Lady Liberty.

There are crowds of people swarming the island, and I'm glad we're on a boat. The air in the city was hot and stagnant, but here on the river, the breeze is perfect. I take a peek at Chase's face as he focuses on the statue. So cute. And so not a jerk. I wonder if he'll try to kiss me again—for the third time—if you count the brush on the lips at the piano. He puts his arm around me and I sink into him. *This is paradise!*

All of a sudden, Dylan pops into my mind, and I feel a little bad, but not too much. I'm sure now I don't want to go out with him when I get back to Texas. I don't think I ever really did. He was the first boy who ever asked me to be his girlfriend, and I said yes, like, automatically. Lady Liberty would never have done that.

And besides, it's true, he wasn't very nice to me.

That settles it. I can take on Mom. I can take on Jas. And as soon as I can, I'll tell Dylan it's over for real. I'm in control of my life! This is the new improved me!

Chase looks down at his watch. "I wish we could sit here forever, but I don't want you to get in trouble. I don't want your Mom to hate me after our first date."

He said date! I sigh out loud. Completely happy. I don't even care if I get in trouble. "My Mom would never hate you!" I say. *And she doesn't even know I'm with you.*

"What about your boyfriend? Dillard?" Chase laughs.

"Dylan." My face turns red.

"I know. I'm teasing. You just made him up, anyway, didn't you? "

I swallow hard. "Um, no. I do…I mean I *did* have a boyfriend named Dylan, but we're not together anymore."

"When did you break up?"

My heart pounds and I can feel my face burning. "Well… um… before I came here this summer." *That's kind of true, right?*

Chase is quiet, and I wish I knew what he was thinking.

"I'm sorry, Lily. All this time I thought you were just kidding. I guess I'm a jerk."

"It's okay. It wasn't working out." I want to change the subject so I throw one back on him. "What about *your* girlfriend? You can't tell me that picture in your dressing room was really your sister!" I try to be funny. "Who carries around a picture of their sister!"

"Lily, that really *is* my sister. Okay?"

He sounds so serious I decide to drop it. I'm not sure I believe it but if he says so...

Chase pulls me in tighter and kisses the top of my hair. "We have to go. I wish we didn't."

In the cab on the way back to the library, Chase holds my hand again but doesn't try to kiss me. He doesn't say anything about when I'll see him again, either. I want to ask, but I remember what Mom told me about appearing desperate with boys. Mom is probably wrong about a lot of things, but not this one. I've seen what happens when girls get all serious the first time a guy pays them any attention. It's pathetic. I'm not that girl. No way.

When we get close to the library, Chase gives me a hug. "That was fun." He smiles at me.

I breathe deep. "You're leaving tomorrow?" I try to sound nonchalant.

"Birmingham, Alabama," Chase says with a fake redneck accent.

"Sounds great to me!" I say, thinking it would be my kind of place—my kind of people. "I don't mean great that you're leaving. I mean... I don't care... but..."

Chase leans over and kisses me on the cheek. "I'll see you in two weeks. In Paris."

"Right," I say. I should just keep my mouth shut. I am so not good at this. I look at my watch. Six twenty.

Please let Curtis be late. I ask the cabbie to stop a block shy of the library so Curtis doesn't see us. "I've gotta run!" I say. "Good luck in Birmingham!" I put my hand on the door, but Chase stops me.

"Lily, if you ever hear or read anything about me that bothers you—promise you'll ask me about it first. Okay?"

I think it's kind of a weird thing to say, but he is a pop star, after all. "Sure," I say and fly out the door.

I run down the street toward the library. If Curtis is already waiting for me, I'll tell him I got bored and went for a walk. But my clothes are different! Ah, he's a man. He'll never notice. I pull a tissue out of my bag and start wiping the make-up off my face. I stumble on part of the sidewalk that's sticking up and almost fall. I can see Chase watching me from the back of the cab, now stopped in traffic in front of the library. I wave and turn away, embarrassed, searching wildly for Curtis. He's just coming around the corner.

I fly into the backseat. "Hi!" I say breathlessly. "Just went for a little walk when I didn't see you!"

"I've been circling this block for half an hour," Curtis says, but not like it bothered him a bit. I think I'm safe. I mean, why should Curtis care what I do?

"Do we have to pick up Mom?" I try to sound casual. She *would* notice my change in wardrobe.

"Not now. She said to drop you at the apartment first. She's in the middle of something." He looks at me in the rearview mirror. "Are you okay?"

"I'm fine!" I say cheerfully. "Nice library!" I lay my head back on the seat, relieved.

"I was looking for a girl in a white T-shirt and jeans. You changed."

"Um…yeah, I spilled coffee on my shirt! Good thing I had an extra one!" Coffee at the library? Extra shirt? Well I *could* have gone to a coffee shop…

Curtis just nods his head and keeps driving.

I've changed all right. I take a deep breath and wonder how I'm ever going to explain this to my sister, and if I even should.

Ten

Who paints the flower, cannot about it paint the odor?

~French proverb

*P*aris! Ah, city of light, city of love. Barf. I hate Paris. Paris is Mom. Everything about her. And I can *so not* be casual and get away with it here. No plain T-shirt and cowboy boots. Not with my mother. My earliest memories of Paris are of Mom putting Jas and me in matching crinoline dresses, Mary Jane shoes, and bows the size of satellite dishes on top our heads. So *not* comfortable. So not *me.* I used to get my clothes all dirty playing in Meme's garden while Jas sat like a little angel on a chair pretending to have tea with the Queen of England.

When I was a kid, I loved Meme's garden and her country home outside of Paris. I loved Meme, too. She was tough, but she understood me. Not like Mom. Everything with Mom is a show. Yes, Meme was rich and proper, too. And I know most of Mom's rules were passed to her through Meme, but somehow, my grandmother was different. She cared about people. Their insides. Somehow I never felt like an embarrassment to her. Like I am to Mom.

We arrived yesterday, among the throngs of tourists who visit Paris every summer. It was hardly better than New York, until we arrived here at Meme's country château. It's almost as good as Texas, minus the horses. At least there are a couple of goats and some chickens. And open space. You can go for a walk and be alone.

I'm lying on a chaise lounge by the pool, soaking in the sun. Lots of green surrounds me. There are flowers everywhere, some in the ground and some in urns. Purple, pink, and white blossoms. I breathe deeply and close my eyes, taking in their scent. So much better than Mom's perfume. Now if Mom could just leave me alone for a few days, I could really enjoy this.

"Don't get too comfortable." Jas's voice jostles me from my Zen-like state. "Mom says we're heading back to Paris this afternoon."

"Why?" I groan. "We just got here." Can't she ever just chill? Just *be?*

Jas lies down on the chaise next to me. "We've been invited to dinner. Some ex-pat viscount, I guess. You know Mom."

"Oh how boorish," I mock. "I can see traveling back to the city for a count, but a viscount? Absurd!"

Jas sighs. Maybe even she's sick of Mom's whirlwind schedule.

"Are we coming back here afterward?" I adjust the back of my chaise and sit up.

"I think so."

"Good. I'll just stay here then."

"Hmm. Not gonna happen. You're the whole reason for the invite."

"What do you mean?"

"Mom said the viscount's wife is an aspiring fashion designer, and she wants you to model a few pieces of her couture line for some magazine spread. Looks like you hit the big time." Jas looks annoyed. She isn't tall enough for runway. Most of her modeling has been for Mom's make-up and some jewelry ads.

"Well, that's too bad," I say. "I did the perfume ad for you, but that's it."

"For *me*? Thanks a lot. You actually ruined my life." Jas brushes a tear from her cheek and puts her head back against the chaise. She squeezes her eyes shut, probably hoping she can make me disappear.

"Jas, I'm sorry…" I can't find the words that will roll back time. Give her back her dream. "I didn't want any of this to happen. You know that."

"Why don't you just quit, then? Tell Mom it's over."

"I wish! We both know *that* isn't going to happen.

Mom would never let this ad campaign crash and burn now." I do feel sorry for Jas. This time Mom has killed two birds—both her daughters—with one stone. "You'll get the next one."

"There will never be an ad campaign to top this one, Lily. You can't do better than Chase Donovan."

There's nothing I can say to that. I want to tell her about Chase and me, but how can I when she's feeling this way?

~~~

On the way back into Paris, I try to enjoy the countryside, but I can't shake the gloom I feel emanating from Jas. Years back, I lost my sister—location wise. If she finds out Chase and I really *are* seeing each other, I could lose her for real.

Are we really seeing each other? He hasn't actually asked me to be his girlfriend. Not the way Dylan did.

Dylan. I *have* to do something about Dylan. Mom's always said it's not right to break up with someone over the phone, but when I get back to New York, that's exactly what I'll have to do. I can't let this go on any longer. Chase or no Chase.

We drive up to a jaw-dropping estate outside of Paris. The iron gates alone are enough to take your breath away. Aristocrats—they really know how to live. The only thing Mom loves more than fortune and fame is nobility. If she could just be royalty, her life would be perfect.

Mom has quizzed us ad nauseam all the way to Lord Whatever's home. Yes, that's how you address a viscount in English, *lord,* and even though *they* speak French, since I barely do anymore, Mom is considering whether or not I should call him that. His wife should be addressed, *Lady Whatever*—if we were in England, which I remind Mom we are not—and his son would *technically* be referred to as The Honorable Blah. But Jas and I will just call him Jacques.

"Haven't you always taught us that titles don't really exist in France?" I ask Mom.

She snorts. "Technically, you are correct. But believe me girls, those who *would* have any right to a title, are nevertheless delighted to be recognized as such." She looks wistfully out the window. "I've met plenty of so called *nobility* who are inferior people. Remember that. *Anyone* can be noble in the truest sense, but only because of what they make of themselves. Certainly not for being born into a family."

As the car makes its way up the long driveway leading to the mansion, I see a guy riding the most beautiful black stallion I've ever seen. The horse's long mane bounces in the breeze, exaggerated by his spirited gait. I could never control a horse like that, and I'm instantly impressed with the guy riding him.

When the car stops, he rides up and dismounts, handing the reigns to a younger boy, who has come out of nowhere to take the horse. Without waiting for someone to open the door for me, I jump out and yell, "Wait!"

Everyone turns and looks at me, including the boy.

"I want to see the horse. Please." I start walking in its direction.

The guy who was riding him steps up and grabs my arm.

"Mademoiselle, he is a dangerous animal. Please let me escort you." He bows and grabs my hand. "I am Jacques Bertrand Davignon. And you are...?"

"Lily."

He bends down and kisses my hand. "It is a pleasure to meet you, Mademoiselle Lily," he says in impeccable English. "Come. Let me introduce you to Monsieur Noir.

Mister Black? How cute.

Jacques leads me to the horse, and then grabs his bridle, whispering to him in French. I stroke his nose gently, and my heart clenches. I miss Fire Star. I miss riding. I fight the urge to throw my arms around his neck and bury my face in his mane.

"He's beautiful."

"Yes, he is." Jacques smiles at me. "You like horses, eh?"

I take my gaze from Monsieur Noir and focus on Jacques. Wow. He's really cute, with dark curly brown hair and big brown eyes. And he's a horse person. Stop right there, Lily! Looking for boyfriend number three? And now gentry? I shake my head. What's wrong with me?

"Uh-hem." I turn and look at Mom and Jas, who are now standing outside the car.

"Madame Laroche..." Jacques hands the reigns back to the younger boy, giving him some instructions in French. "Welcome." He kisses Mom on both cheeks. "And you must be Jasmine." He kisses Jas on both cheeks, too. Offering Mom his arm, he leads us all up to the enormous wood doors in front of the house, just as they are opened by a butler.

The viscount and his wife have obviously been informed of our arrival and are standing in the humongous entry hall to greet us. They're dressed nicely, but much more casually than we are, since Mom made us dress to the nines. I know exactly what she'd say if I commented on the discrepancy. *"You are never overdressed. Other people are underdressed."* We've heard it all our lives. But these people are nobility. And European. Will Mom acknowledge she's forced us to overdress on this occasion? Never.

We're fussed over for several minutes. You've never seen so many kisses. Multiply the number of people by two cheeks, and then add a few extras. Personally, I find it ridiculous. I don't even *know* these people.

And don't even get me started about other French customs. I already know dinner will be at least five courses and last for *hours*. I mean, is all that really necessary? Do we really need a plate of a gazillion cheeses passed around *after* dinner and *before* dessert? I think not.

Before we eat, Jacques gives Jas and me a tour of

the stables. My heels catch on the cobble stone path while Jas walks with all the poise of a queen, despite wearing even higher heels than I have on. I consider removing my shoes, but even I don't go barefoot around horses. Jacques offers me his arm when he sees the difficulty I'm having, and Jas flashes me a dirty look. Is she jealous? It gives me an idea. Maybe if Jas gets interested in Jacques…

The stable is made of the same pale limestone as the mansion, and looks like it's hundreds of years old. Probably is. It's beautiful. I can't help but feel like a little girl when we enter and I see the horses. Just hearing their whinnies makes my heart flutter. I let go of Jacques's arm and practically run to the nearest stall. I hear him chuckle. I turn to look at Jas, who looks like she's trying not to breath. She's never liked barns or the smell of animals. Maybe this isn't such a good idea. She's acting all prissy, and I'm seriously hoping for a match here. Then again, some guys like prissy girls. French guys probably do. I'll just have to hope.

"*Excusez-moi, Mademoiselles.*" Jacques bows to both of us. "I'll be just a moment." He leaves us and discusses something with the younger boy we saw earlier, who is now at the far end of the stable, cleaning some tack. I take the opportunity to work on Jas. *Maybe some reverse psychology?*

"Wow. He's cute. I call dibs," I say, hoping Jas takes the bait.

"Sure," Jas says. "That's only fair, since I already called dibs on Chase."

That went well.

Jacques returns and we continue our tour. After the stables, we walk through a vineyard, a small winery, and then a beautiful garden that looks like a mini-sized version of Versailles. The path through the garden winds back up to the main house, passing a large rectangular pool. Two stone lions sit on either side of a wide staircase leading up to a huge terrace. They remind me of the ones in front of the library in New York, and I miss Chase.

On the terrace there's a large wood table, beautifully set for dinner. Our hostess signals for me to sit between her and Jacques. I pretend I don't understand her and move to the other side of the table next to Mom, forcing Jas to sit by Jacques. Mom looks at me suspiciously. I was probably three the last time I wanted to sit by her.

Here we go. Course number one. And voila! Of course we are served *foie gras* and *escargot*. Yummy? Maybe if you like goose liver and snails. I don't. But I serve myself a tiny bit when the plates are passed around. Ever since I was old enough to sit at a table, I've had to sample everything that's served. Luckily women eat like birds in France, so my tiny portions go unnoticed.

I pick up the little tool used to hold snail shells in place, so I can take the little piece of slime out. It suddenly reminds me of the eyelash curler Gaston uses on my lashes before applying fifty coats of mascara. I'll never forget when Mom first taught Jas and me to use one of these escargot thingies. I must've been four or five. I remember crying as Mom forced me to sit at the table until I ate a snail. Jas had eaten hers right away—always obedient—always wanting to please Mom. I remember, too, that Daddy was out of town. I was sure he would have saved me—would've told Mom to leave me alone. It was one of Mom's many victories. Well, she can make me eat a snail, but she can't force me to like it.

After the main course, we're served salad. That's another crazy thing about France—you have to be an expert in origami to eat lettuce. You have to take your fork and fold the lettuce leaves up until they'll fit in your mouth. Cutting lettuce with a knife is absolutely *not done*. It's been a while, so it takes me forever to fold up the first one. *Forget it, I'm cutting this sucker!* I pick up my knife and make the mistake of looking at Mom. I can read her mind—it's something along the lines of *drop that knife or I'll stab you with it.* I drop the knife.

I manage to fold and eat most of my salad, looking forward to dessert. I love French desserts! But first we have to eat cheese. I have to admit I like French cheeses, too. Even the strong smelly ones. The butler stands holding the plate of cheeses by my side. "Mademoiselle." He bows slightly. I scan the platter. "Merci," I reply, and take a small slice of the *Brie de Meaux*. I see Mom nod her approval.

Mom and the aristocrats have been babbling the whole time in French, and I realize just how rusty I am. I bob my head and smile every once in awhile and add an occasional *oui*. I notice Jas and Jacques have had a few private conversations in English during dinner. Maybe there's a spark after all.

"I am so happy you have agreed to model my clothing," Madame Davignon says to me in English.

It's a done deal? I haven't even seen her clothes yet. Instead of answering, I give her what I hope comes off as a smile, because it doesn't feel like one. When did this happen? I want to glare at Mom, but she doesn't look my way.

After dessert, which is a delicious chocolate soufflé, Madame Davignon instructs one of her servants to retrieve her sketch book. The first drawing she shows us is ridiculous, and I promise I'm being nice. *Please don't make me wear that.* The only way I can describe it is a cross between a cavewoman and a peacock. They get worse. Mom oohs and aahs over each one.

Jas loves couture, but I can see her smirking. These are terrible! I swear even Jacques flashes me a look of sympathy. The adults plan the photo shoot in French, and I can only make out half of what they're saying. "*Ces sont belles,*" Mom says. That I know. "These are lovely." She can't really mean that.

"Do you like?" Madame Davignon suddenly asks me in her broken English. She is grinning from ear to ear.

"Um..." I glance at Mom who is shooting me daggers. "They're...they're...very *unique*," I answer. Inside, I'm steaming. I am *not* modeling those clothes.

I look at Mom. She has that look on her face. The one she gets when the whole world is going her way, which it usually is. Well, she's going to be disappointed when I tell her I won't do it.

At least Jas is now flirting shamelessly with Jacques. "Will you be coming to the photo shoot tomorrow?" she asks him, resting her hand on his forearm.

"If you are there, I am there," he answers, resting his hand on hers for a brief second. Oh, that's cozy. My plan is so working. I'm going to tell her about Chase and me tonight, when we get back to the château. Better yet, I'll tell both Jas and Mom on the drive back. I close my eyes and picture Lady Liberty. I can do this! And I'm even going to tell Mom that I refuse to model those clothes.

The good-byes are as ridiculous as the hellos. Kissy, kissy, kissy. I see Jacques linger a little longer than necessary when he kisses Jas. He takes her hand and says, "*Au revoir, ma bichette.*" I'm startled for a second, but then remember it means *my little doe.* It takes a while to get used to terms of endearment in French. Meme used to call me *ma petit crotte,* which means *my droppings,* and also *little round goat cheese,* and yes, that's a compliment.

Jas looks up at him through her eyelashes and smiles. A future viscount might trump a pop star, after all. Isn't that just a few hops and skips away from a prince?

Jacques is gorgeous, but for me, he can't compare to Chase. And I don't mean in the looks department, because everyone knows Chase is adorable. There's just something about Chase. He's goofy. And kind. And so sweet. I close my eyes and picture his smile. It makes me happy.

On the way back, I wait until we've been driving for a while and then make my move. "Hey Mom, I've been thinking . . . that clothing line isn't really me, you know." I chuckle all friendly like. "I think I'll skip it."

"Don't be ridiculous. I've already finished the negotiations." Mom raises her chin and crosses her arms. "We'll run a perfume ad in the same magazine."

"But I don't like those clothes... they're..."

"Models don't model what they *like*, Lily; they model what they are *hired* to model. Period."

"But I'm not a model."

"You are now. At least until the *Royale* campaign is finished. Having you model couture in a French fashion magazine simultaneously will be icing on the cake. We've already been receiving orders for *Royale* all over Europe." Mom grins. "Securing Chase Donovan for this ad campaign was genius." She tosses her head and stares straight ahead, signaling the end to our conversation.

I want to blurt out that I'm seeing Chase, but doubt rises up and squashes me. We spent a few hours together. He never *said* it was anything more. What if it's not? Why start a drama fest with Jas? Maybe I should wait and tell her when and if I absolutely have to.

So much for being brave. I might as well call myself Lady Loser-ty. I sit back in silence.

Couture, here I come.

Eleven

Good perfume is known by its scent rather than by the perfumer's advertisement. ~Afghan Proverb

No. This can't be happening! I gape at my reflection in the mirror in front of me. My hair has been teased to a full eight inches above my head and sprayed to the consistency of nylon rope. Immovable. My eyes are surrounded by giant sweeps of charcoal eyeliner. Centimeters thick. But that's nothing compared to what I'm wearing. It's the peacock-cavewoman ensemble. There's a strip of silver and black cheetah-print silk across my chest, and yes—feathers—barely covering my bum. Forget the peacock, I feel more like an ostrich, and I wish I could find a hole in the ground to bury my head.

"Fabulous!" Mom exclaims when I step outside the tent.

We're shooting in an urban setting—an ugly urban setting—complete with graffiti and a white makeshift tent converted to an on-site make-up studio and dressing room. With all the beautiful neighborhoods and landmarks in Paris, they've chosen something "edgy." My beauty and the beauty of the clothes in contrast to the grunge. That's what I was told anyway.

Mom prefers to pretend these neighborhoods don't exist. She favors the historic, the opulent. But you would never guess it by her performance here today. She's glowing.

The photographer instructs me to stand in front of a graffiti covered cement wall. The heels I'm wearing look like medieval torture devices with more straps than a horse's bridle and the highest spiky heels I've ever seen. I stumble over to the wall and brace myself against it so I don't fall.

"Crouch down, Lily," he says. "Like this." He contorts his body into a ridiculous pose that makes his butt stick out behind him. Does he not notice I'm wearing feathers? I'll look like a duck if I do that. I crouch half-way down but that's not enough for him. "More, Lily. Lower. Lower."

I bend my knees as far as I can without losing my balance. It hurts. It has to look stupid. I glance at Mom for support. She wouldn't want to ruin the Laroche name with an embarrassing spread in a fashion magazine, would she? Surely, she'll rescue me.

"Lower," the photographer barks again.

"Lily. Are you an imbecile?" Mom snarls. "Do exactly as he says. Now."

Tears wet my eyes, but I fight them fiercely. If the charcoal around them starts to drip, I'll look like a zombie, or worse—a clown.

I guess I am a clown. Mom's puppet, nothing more.

I crouch down and stick my butt out behind me.

"Your face!" the photographer shouts. "Your body looks unnatural and the expression on your face is…is…" He waves one hand in the air. "You look… *constipé!*"

Constipated? Great. I look around for Jasmine. She and Jacques are a part of our entourage, but now, I see neither. I could really use some help here.

I feel tears welling up, threatening to spill over. I squeeze my eyes shut—trying to summon enough strength to stand up for myself.

"I can't do this, Mom. I won't."

I stop crouching. Everyone stops and stares at me, like they didn't hear me right. I walk in the direction of the tent, pulling at the feathers to make sure no one sees something they're not supposed to.

"These spoiled American models!" The photographer gestures wildly with his hands. *"Incorrigible!"*

I expect Mom to scream at me. To grab me and force me to go back, but she doesn't. I can't believe I am being allowed to walk away. I pick up my pace toward the tent and stumble over my shoes. Jacques is suddenly there beside me, holding me up. I can't look at his face. Instead, I turn my gaze toward Madame Davignon. She's completely silent, but her eyes are wide with confusion.

Jas stands in front of me. "What are you doing, Lily? You can't just walk away from this." Her voice is barely a whisper.

Jacques remains at my side, quietly holding my arm. Calm and patient.

I take a deep breath. "Help me, Jas. Please."

"The straps aren't right on these shoes," Jas announces boldly to everyone. "We need a wardrobe adjustment." She takes my other arm and strides the rest of the way back to the tent, pulling me along. "Please give us a few moments, Madame Davignon." Jas smiles at her and reassures her, then firmly but politely orders everyone from the tent, including Jacques.

I hobble to a chair and burst into tears.

"Stop it. Now!" Jas grabs my shoulders. "It's not that bad. Listen to me. You'll ruin your make up." She grabs a tissue off the make-up table and hands it to me. "You must not cry."

She kneels down in front of me and tightens all the straps on the torture shoes. "It might hurt a little, but it will help you walk. The tighter the better. Now look at me. You can do this."

"I don't want to do this."

"It's too late for that, now."

"But I can't. Did you see me out there? The guy said I looked constipated."

Jas suppresses a giggle. "Sorry. But that is kind of funny."

I glare at her, then giggle too. "What am I going to do, Jas?"

"I'll help you. Just like we did at the studio in New York." Jas stands up. "Remember, it all comes from inside. Think beautiful—be beautiful."

"But this outfit—this make-up—is uug-lee."

"But *you're* beautiful. You can make anything look good. C'mon."

Jas pulls me up from the chair and leads me out of the tent. "We're ready now," she announces to no one in particular.

Mom hasn't moved from the area where the cameras are set up. She's deep in conversation with Lady Davignon, completely nonplussed.

The straps of my shoes are practically digging into my skin, but Jas was right, it's so much easier to walk. "Get an attitude on, girl," she whispers as we stride toward the set. "You're hot."

I'm hot. I try not to choke. *I'm beautiful.* I keep walking toward the wall. I throw my shoulders back. I feel stupid, but force myself into character. Like an actress. It's the only way I'll get through this. I'll do this one more time, and then I'll tell Mom I quit. One. More. Time.

Jas has a word with the photographer. I wish I had her poise, her confidence. She jokes with him in French and I make out something about letting me move more naturally, until I get the hang of it. Jacques watches her with admiration.

The photographer is as sweet as sugar as he turns back to me. "Let's begin again, *ma petit.*"

Jas makes some glamorous poses behind the photographer. She looks elegant and stunning as she moves effortlessly, showing me what to do. I try to imitate her as best I can.

"Much better." The photographer begins clicking, and I meld my thoughts and emotions into what I am supposed to be. The real me disappears into the ground, like molten lava.

"A little sad, *triste,*" he says, "but *très belle.* Beautiful." *Click. Click.*

Twelve

"The odor of pink, low, thanks to the light wind of summer that passes, mixes with the perfumes that it put." ~Paul Verlaine

J'm standing in front of a three-way mirror in the dress shop of one of Mom's favorite *petits couturiers, Sophie,* trying on the princess gown for my Sweet Sixteen. I'd like to say I hate it. I should hate it. I'm a cowgirl, a tomboy. But it's pretty. Really pretty!

I thought Mom would have ordered pale blue, like Cinderella's dress in the Disney movie, but it's pink. And cream. And gold, too. When I was a little girl, I was fascinated by the pink dress the birds and the mice made Cinderella in the attic. It was my favorite color. And I loved that her little animal friends made it just for her. I was devastated when her stepsisters ripped it up. But after Mom and Jas moved away, I removed all pink from my life. All things girly-girl.

The dress seems to fit me perfectly and probably only needs to be hemmed. I turn and look at all sides. It's everything you could imagine it to be. Like it was taken directly from a French princess during the Renaissance. I feel beautiful in it. I imagine Chase dressed as a prince, holding his hand out to me and taking a bow.

I catch myself smiling in the mirror and quickly look to see if Mom is watching. She's examining her own dress that's hanging on a rack. It's all gold. A light shimmery gold. Totally Hya. I can't let Mom know I actually love my dress. She doesn't deserve the satisfaction.

"Well, you've done an excellent job on this one." Mom stands behind me, examining my gown. "It's exquisite."

Sophie looks right at my face in the mirror. "Do you like it, Mademoiselle?"

I straighten the flounce on each side and look at myself again. I stand up straight, and then I make the mistake of looking at Mom's reflection. "I…"

"Of course she likes it!" Mom's forceful voice drowns mine out. "I want it taken in slightly here," Mom says, tugging on the bodice at the smallest part of my waist. "And a little at the shoulders."

Sophie's eyes meet mine before she slides in a pin at the exact spot where Mom was pointing. I look down. I want to tell Sophie how much I really do like it, but I can't.

Jas emerges from the dressing room in her gown and waits for me to get off the platform. Her dress is an emerald green. Stunning. I think for a moment that green is the color of envy. But that's not Jas. She's never been envious of anyone. Until now?

"I love it!" Jas singsongs, smiling at her reflection in the mirror. I wonder if Mom consulted Jas first, or if Mom just had the dress made, like she did mine.

"I told you this color would suit me, Mother." Jas puts her hands on her waist and turns from side to side. I guess that answers my question.

"It certainly does. My concern was the season, Jasmine. The color is a little dark for New York in July." Mom clicks her tongue. "But it is a costume party, so I'll allow it."

Will you allow cowboy boots with mine? I bite my lip and step off the platform. "You look gorgeous, Jas."

"I know!" Jas steps up on the platform and twirls. "The only thing missing is a tiara!"

A tiara? Puh-leez.

"It's Lily's party. She'll be the only one wearing a tiara." Mom purses her lips.

"I'm not wearing a tiara," I say.

"Don't be ridiculous, Lily. The theme is Cinderella. Cinderella is a princess. Princesses wear tiaras. End of discussion." Mom raises her chin.

"I'm her sister. If she's a princess, I'm a princess. I

should be able to wear a tiara, too." Jas puts her hands on her hips and stares down Mom. Sometimes she's all guts.

"It's okay, Mom. She can wear a tiara. I don't have to be the star attraction."

"Of course you do. It's your Sweet Sixteen. You're the *Royale* Perfume Princess." Mom waves her hand and walks back to her dress. We've been dismissed.

Jas tries again. "How about a smaller one than Lily's?" Oh great. Does that mean Mom is going to find me a ridiculous, giant CROWN?

Mom doesn't even acknowledge the question, which is Hya code for I'm going to pretend you didn't ask that. She reexamines her dress. "Sophie, we really must discuss this sash."

End of royal discussion.

I can only pray my tiara is not monstrous. That I couldn't bear.

"You can change now, Miss Lily." Sophie touches my arm.

"Thank you," I say quietly, and then add, "I really like my dress."

The room is all mirrors. I see one of Mom's eyebrows raise as I swish my way into the dressing room. Hya wins again.

Thirteen

"The perfumes are full with stratagems and if you treat them with negligence, they scatter your secrecies with the four winds." ~Louise de Vilmorin

Chase is coming today! I haven't seen or spoken to him in two weeks. If he really *is* my boyfriend, he's not very attentive. But I guess it would be hard for him to get a hold of me here, even though he could find a way if he tried hard enough. I need to talk to Mom about getting my cell phone back. She has no reason to worry about Dylan anymore.

We've moved our things back to the apartment in Paris, to be close to the shoot tomorrow, and to entertain Chase and his mom when they get here today. Usually leaving the country and going into Paris depresses me, but I'm singing and dancing around the flat. I feel good! Except when I think about Jas finding out about Chase. I have to tell her—like now—before he gets here.

I take one of my new sundresses out of my suitcase and hang it in the closet. It's a sunshiny yellow, and I think I'll wear it today when I see Chase. To remind him of Texas, you know, the whole yellow rose of Texas thing. I've got the windows and the double doors to the balcony open. The wrought iron railing looks beautiful against the robin-egg blue sky and the white fluffy clouds. I can see a faint silhouette of the Eiffel tower in the distance. Tomorrow I'll be posing on it—with Chase! I twirl on the marble floor and do a little jump.

"What's wrong with you?" Jas comes into the room, dragging her suitcase behind her. We share this room whenever we're in Paris. There are two matching, iron twin beds, and Jas plops down on hers. "Are you on something?"

"No, just happy!" *Should I tell her now?*

"Is it because Chase is coming today?"

"No! Of course not." *What?* Okay. Deep breath. Do it. *Now.* "Uh…"

"Do you think he'll like this dress?" Jas pulls a sheer baby-blue sundress out of a garment bag and holds it up under her chin.

Crap. Double crap.

"Jas…" She has to know, doesn't she? Chase asked *me* to dance in front of her. He took *me* somewhere quiet to talk. Does she need someone to spell it out for her? "Um... remember that night at Ciao..."

"Oh, don't worry, Lily. I'm over it. I mean, what could you do, right? You were probably caught off guard." Jas drapes the blue sundress on the bed and takes her make-up bag out of her suitcase.

"Ladies." Mom strides into the room. "What are we wearing tonight? Let's decide now."

Jas looks at me and rolls her eyes behind Mom's back. "I've got it covered, Mom."

"What about you, Lily?" Mom unzips one of the garment bags on my bed.

Do I have a choice?

She rapidly lays my clothing in a row along the bed. "Definitely, this." Mom holds up a ruffled white cotton sundress. The one I hate. I hate ruffles. But it is kind of romantic... Maybe Chase would like it?

"Fine," I huff. "With what shoes?"

"These silver Marc Jacob sandals, of course."

Mom calls them sandals. In my mind, real sandals don't have three-inch heels. Good thing Chase is tall. I'll be towering over everybody else.

"What about these?" I take a pair of white flat sandals with some pretty rhinestones on them out of my suitcase and show Mom.

"We aren't going to the *beach*." Mom takes a step toward the door. "Jasmine, come with me to the market. I want to pick out some flowers."

"Sure." Jas stops unpacking. "Can we stop at Lou Lou's? I really need a latte."

"You know what too much caffeine does to your skin. But, yes, we'll stop at Lou Lou's."

"You coming?" Jas looks at me.

"No," Mom commands. "Lily, I want you to start getting ready for this evening. We'll be meeting Chase and his mother at their hotel around six. The paparazzi will be thick as thieves. You have to look perfect. I want you to take a bath, wash your hair and let it air dry."

"Um… it's only like two p.m.," I say. I don't want to go to the market with Mom, but c'mon. Do I really need to start getting ready this early?

"Beauty takes time. I thought you would realize that by now. What would you like from Lou Lou's? We'll bring you something back." Mom looks at me impatiently.

"One of those croissants with the chocolate inside."

Mom sighs. "Very well, but you're a model now. No eating between meals. You may have it for breakfast tomorrow."

I know Mom doesn't believe in snacking, and I hardly ever do, but she's never actually stopped me. I guess she didn't care before. If this is how Moms cares about someone, I'd rather she didn't. The good mood I had earlier has evaporated. I want to go home. To Texas. To Dad. I'd take a piece of cornbread instead.

"And use that mask I gave you yesterday. I can see your pores." Mom strides out of the room. "Let's go, Jasmine. Before all the best flowers are gone."

Jas gives me a sympathetic look as she slips her sandals on and follows Mom out the door. "Welcome to my world," she mouths.

Fourteen

"Indulgence is like the perfume of the truth."

~Anne-Sophie Swetchine

On the way to Chase's hotel, I panic. I've had two whole weeks to tell Mom and Jas about Chase, but I'm a coward. Maybe they won't notice. I mean, it's not like he'll announce it to the press or anything the moment he sees me. I take a deep breath. It will all work out. *Won't it?*

We're taking two identical black Mercedes to Chase's hotel. The three of us sit in the back of one, with a French driver and Curtis in the front. The other car contains three more bodyguards Mom hired. Seems like overkill to me.

I'm wearing the white dress Mom picked out, of

course. And the heels. But after the torture devices I wore for Lady Davignon's photo shoot, these don't seem so bad. My hair is styled almost the same way it was that day at Bergdorf's, with long, soft, spiraling curls. I was surprised Mom had the stylist keep my make-up on the light side, for a more natural effect. I have to admit, it's not a bad look for my first meeting with Chase in two weeks—except I still wish I was wearing the yellow dress.

"The European paparazzi are just as bad—or even worse—than those in the States. You both need to be prepared," Mom lectures. I'm sitting in the middle, between Mom and Jas. Trapped. Like a raccoon up a tree with a couple of dogs at the bottom.

"Jasmine," Mom continues, "I know you had your heart set on dating Chase, but remember, for appearances, we must make it look like he's with Lily." She crosses her ankles and sits up straight. "It's business."

Jas looks out the window. "Great, Mom. Ruin my life some more."

"It's not so bad. Why don't you invite Jacques Davignon to dinner tomorrow night? He's charming. And need I mention he's the titled heir to a viscount? Heir to one of the richest men in all of Europe?" Mom pushes back her huge sunglasses. "Really, Jas. This is a no brainer."

"What about Lily's *real* boyfriend, Mom? Ever think about how *he* might feel about this?" Jas slouches against the seat.

Mom snorts. "Lily is finished with him. Aren't

you, Lily?"

My old self would have denied it, would have stuck up for Dylan out of principle, but maybe I should try the truth. "Actually, I am... and..."

Jas interrupts. "Wow. Little Miss Cowgirl is finally joining the ranks. Well guess what? Chase is not really your boyfriend. Don't forget it. Make it perfectly clear to him that this is business. And as soon as this ad campaign is over—he's mine. *Comprenez-vous?*"

I'm not used to my sister talking to me like this. She never has. I can understand the jealousy. This was supposed to be her job, but why take it out on me?

"You're lucky I kind of like Jacques—for now." Jas leans around me and says to Mom. "Did you know he's going to your and Dad's alma mater in the fall?"

"Oh that's great," I say. "This time it will be a Texas *girl* falling in love with a French *boy* at Columbia. Only maybe this time it will work out. You're *both* snobs!"

"I'm not going to Columbia." Jas raises her chin.

Wow. That's the part that bothers her? "Of course you're not. You have to *study* to get in. Do you have any idea how hard it is to get accepted?" I shake my head.

"Whatever." Jas won't look at me.

"Both of you stop this nonsense," Mom says. "There are plenty of colleges, and plenty of boys to go around. Focus on the task at hand."

And what's that? Sell perfume? I fold my arms and look out Mom's window. I'm done worrying about Jas. If this is how she wants to be—fine. Suddenly, a guy on a motorcycle pulls up alongside us and stares right at me. A huge camera hangs around his neck. Our windows are dark, so he probably can't see me as well as I can see him. It freaks me out.

"Well, they've found us," Mom says, none too disappointed. "Let that be the end to your bickering." She pulls out a compact and checks her lipstick, then adds another layer. Hya Laroche is never, and I mean *never*, seen without lipstick.

We pull up to the Hotel de Crillon, which is virtually surrounded by paparazzi.

"Just smile and nod," Mom instructs. "Don't get sucked into their questioning."

We wait for the bodyguards from the other car to get out and stand near our door. The one that rode in the front seat of our car gets out, opens our door, and then helps us onto the curb, while the others block the paparazzi from getting too close.

"Jasmine!" One yells. "Is your career over with Laroche cosmetics?" Jas keeps her head down and walks straight toward the door of the hotel.

I swallow hard. No wonder no one likes paparazzi. I know I'm supposed to ignore them, but brat or no brat—I have to defend my sister. "Of course not!" I turn and confront them. "She's the face of Laroche Cosmetics."

"And you're the body?" Another cackles. They all laugh.

"That's very rude!" I shout as their cameras flash.

Mom rushes me into the hotel lobby. She doesn't look happy. And I can't tell whether Jas wants to laugh or cry.

"Well, that will definitely make the tabloids." Mom grimaces. "Listen to me, Lily. They may be annoying, but you must behave appropriately. If you don't, they *will* destroy you."

"Did you hear what they said?"

"Yes, and they wouldn't have said it if you hadn't stepped into their trap to begin with."

I gulp. She's right. Again.

We are led into a sitting room adjacent to a private dining area, where I'm guessing we'll have dinner. My heart pounds. Finally, after all this time, I'm going to see Chase! I take a deep breath. He's already in the room, standing in a corner, talking to his mom.

As soon as we enter, he looks over, and our eyes meet. I feel myself melt into those smiling, deep-into-your-soul, dark blue eyes. He crosses the room in seconds, going straight for me. "Lily!" He lifts me up in a big bear hug and we both laugh. My heart flutters.

He kisses both my cheeks, the French way, and then kisses Mom and Jas while I say hello to Mrs. Donovan. She gives me a big hug, too, and something tells me she knows. Chase probably doesn't have to keep secrets from *her*, not like I have to with my mom.

If Jas has noticed anything suspicious about our greeting, she's not letting on.

I sit next to Chase at the table and every once in a

while he squeezes my hand. I wonder what Jas is thinking. There are no paparazzi in here. No need for a show. Is my secret out? She's probably wondering: *when and where did this happen?* My happiness at being with Chase is ruined by the realization that I've betrayed my sister. My only sister. The sister I have loved and idolized my entire life.

"How was Alabama?" I ask Chase, trying to hide my nerves.

"Great. That seems so long ago. I've toured six cities since then." He holds my hand. "How's it going here in Paris?"

"Terrible. My mom forced me to model the most horrible clothing line you could ever imagine. Wait till you see the pictures." I nonchalantly pull my hand away, pretending I need to scratch an imaginary itch on my arm.

"They must be beautiful. Any picture of you has to be." He takes my hand again.

I have to tell Jas now—right now—before this gets any more obvious. "I'll be right back." I stand up and stumble over my chair.

Chase gets up and steadies me, holding on to my arm. He pulls my chair back.

"Ladies' room," I whisper and smile.

I walk over to Jas's chair and lean down. "Will you come to the bathroom with me? I need to talk to you." My heart is pounding.

"You're about the last person I want to speak to right now."

"Please, Jas. It's important."

She resumes her discussion with Chase's manager, ignoring me completely.

"Jasmine, please. It's urgent."

"I said no," she hisses at me, and then turns and smiles. Just like Mom.

I go to the ladies' room alone and sit for awhile in the lounge, trying to work out a plan. There has to be a way to make Jas understand. I wanted to tell her. I tried to tell her. I just couldn't.

I don't want Chase to wonder what I'm doing so long in the bathroom, so I go back to the table. I'll have to make it look like Chase and I are just friends until I get a chance to tell Jas the truth.

When I get back to the table, I'm glad to see the main course has already been served. Filet Mignon—or as we say back in Texas—steak. I decide to eat it the European way and keep both of my hands busy, and therefore out of Chase's reach. I hold my meat down with the fork in my left hand while I cut it with the knife in my right, like we do in the States. But then instead of putting the knife down and switching the fork to my right hand, I put the piece of steak directly in my mouth using my left. It's a little hard to do, but it keeps a utensil in both of my hands at all times. I get busy on my steak and break Mom's rule about putting your silverware down and resting between bites. She gives me the evil eye from across the table. "Breathe," she mouths to me and rolls her eyes.

"Hungry?" Chase smiles.

I nod my head and push a piece of steak against my cheek, missing my mouth. I take aim again and this time hit the target.

Mom clears her throat from across the table. "Chase, would you like to take a cruise down the Seine tomorrow night? Your mother was telling me that the two of you have never been on one. It's quite beautiful."

He looks at me like he wants my approval, which is really sweet. I nod my head.

"That would be great, Mrs. Laroche." Chase smiles at her, and then at me. So adorable.

"Please—call me Hya," Mom drawls.

I choke a little on my food.

"Are you okay?" Chase puts his hand on my back, and I tense up.

I nod and keep on chewing.

"Are you sure everything's all right? You seem upset." Chase is even more adorable when he looks concerned. I wish I could hug him right now.

"I'm fine," I say, hoping I sound convincing. This is so not Chase's fault. He doesn't even know Jasmine likes him. And I can't tell him she does, either. That would be a double betrayal—and double embarrassing for Jas.

"All these paparazzi outside make me a little nervous, that's all." I give Chase a little smile, hoping it doesn't look as fake as I feel.

"I don't blame you. It's the one thing I never get

used to." Chase removes his hand from my back and takes a bite of food.

I exhale. "I don't want to get used to it, you know? I just want to be normal again." Immediately, I regret my words. Chase's eyes change from concerned to almost sad. He doesn't have a choice any more. He'll either become a has-been and be left alone, or remain popular and be constantly harassed. I think my comment confused him, but how do I explain that I don't know what's become of my life—or that I haven't even told anyone we're dating?

My steak is nearly gone, but hey, it's not even half the size of the steak they serve in Texas. Now what? I fold my hands in my lap and stare straight ahead. I must have sent Chase the message because he keeps his hands to himself.

"Can we go for a walk after dinner?" Chase asks me. "Just the two of us?"

You mean the two of us and a brigade of body guards? "Do you really think that's a good idea with all the paparazzi outside?" Actually, there is nothing I'd like more than to be alone with Chase, but not until I've told Jas the truth.

Mom has obviously been listening, because she barges in on our conversation. "You've had a dreadfully long flight, and the shoot's early tomorrow. I suggest we let you and your mother rest. Maybe we could take a stroll along the streets in Montmartre after dinner tomorrow, before our river cruise. Have you ever been to

Montmartre, Chase? It's delightful."

"No, I haven't, but I heard it's really nice." Chase sighs. He probably doesn't know who is more difficult— Mom or me. "Lily, how can I get a hold of you? You're still without a phone? Can you give me Jasmine's number, so I can call you?"

Even though Jas is across the table and three people down from us, her ears are like radar. She perks right up. "Pass me your phone, Chase, and I'll add it for you." She smiles and bats her eyes at him. "Lily and I are always together. Aren't we Lily?"

"Uh-huh." I nod my head, which is now pounding.

Jas takes Chase's phone and types in her number, then smiles and gives it back to him. "Call anytime," she says sweetly and then turns her fake smile on me. My blood pressure is rising by the minute. How can I get out of this mess? I think about Dad and know just what he would say. *Tell the truth, Lily. The truth will set you free.*

Okay, Dad. I will.

Just as soon as I get the chance.

Maybe right after dessert—and the cheese, of course.

The waiter sets my dessert in front of me. It's a small chocolate molten cake. I've had it here before, and it's probably my favorite dessert in all of France—maybe in the entire world—but today I can't enjoy it. I start to sweat. The only thing between me and doomsday is the cheese.

In obedience to Hya's rules, Jas cuts her dessert in half. Personally, I think leaving half a molten cake from the Hotel Crillon uneaten is an international crime. I eat the whole thing in tiny slow bites.

Here comes the cheese. Gulp.

"Mademoiselle," the waiter says, displaying the cheeses in front of me. I take several slices—totally taboo—and Mom glares at me. I cut into a piece of deeply veined blue cheese and eat it as slowly as I possibly can. It's going to give me bad breath, but I need more time to get up my courage.

As soon as she finishes one ultra-thin slice of Roquefort, Jas gets up and sits in an empty chair next to Chase. I guess she's ready to take matters into her own hands. *Help!*

"When will your tour be over?" Jas tosses her hair back and leans in toward Chase.

"September."

"It must be exhausting—traveling so much." Jas places a beautifully French manicured hand on the table near Chase's arm and looks him in the eyes. "How does your girlfriend stand you being gone so much?"

I think Jas is trying to see if that photo we saw in his dressing room at the concert was really a girlfriend he hides from the public. Whew! Maybe I've dodged another bullet.

Chase looks at her quizzically and then laughs. "You should know!"

Uh-oh.

Jas looks equally confused. "I've never had a boyfriend who travels so much—I mean—I don't even have a boyfriend…right now."

"Well, since Lily and I have really only had one date so far…"

No, no, no!

"…I guess it's too early to tell how much she's going to hate it." Chase puts his arm around me. "Huh, Lily? Have you missed me yet?"

Jas raises her eyebrows and looks at me expectantly. I gulp. I open my mouth to speak, but before anything comes out, Jas throws her head back and laughs. Hard.

"Oh Chase, you're hilarious! You're sure taking this perfume ad seriously. I've got to hand it to you—you got me on that one!"

Does Jas think the "one date" Chase is talking about is the ad campaign at Bergdorf's? I look at Chase who seems more confused than ever.

"Sorry to put an end to this lively conversation," Mom interrupts, "but we must be going. We'll see Chase and Mrs. Donovan early in the morning." Jas gives Mom the evil eye, but Mom ignores her. "Chase, it's been a pleasure. Girls…"

We each give Chase a hug. He squeezes my hand and whispers, "Are you sure everything's okay?"

"Yes." *Um, no.*

"I'll call you on Jas's phone—in a little while." Chase looks hopeful.

"No! I mean, that's not a good idea."

"Why, Lily?"

"I don't mind, Chase. Call anytime!" Jas throws herself in between us.

"Let's go, girls," Mom prods.

"*Au revoir!*" Jas singsongs.

I look back and give Chase a tiny wave, hoping he can read my eyes. *I'm sorry. I do like you. Please believe me.*

The bodyguards take us past the paparazzi, and this time I don't say a word, no matter how many times they shout my name. We get in the car and as soon as we pull away the rodeo begins. Jas is more fired up than a bull in the starting pen.

"You have a lot of explaining to do, Lily!" She glares at me, waiting for my answer.

"I tried to tell you…"

Mom grabs me by the arm and puts a finger to her lips. She gestures with her head to the front seat. Another rule, of course, no arguing in front of the help. I remember everything we said on the way to the restaurant. I guess Mom realizes the driver probably knows enough English to expose the entire Lily/Chase dating charade to the public—even though she has every person who does even the smallest job for us sign a ten-page confidentiality contract.

"Whatever you two have to discuss, you will do it in private," Mom grits her teeth and drops my arm.

I steal a peek at Jas. Her eyes are angry and confused. I'm such a jerk.

We ride back to the flat in complete silence. Jas stares out the window, but I can see her hands shaking. I go over in my mind what I'm going to say, how I'll make everything right again. She has to forgive me. *Doesn't she?* I'm her sister.

Jas manages to compose herself as we enter the building and go upstairs, but as soon as we enter the flat, she lunges for me, pushing me down on the couch. "You traitor!"

"Jasmine! Stop this instant!" Mom grabs Jas from behind. "Calm down."

"I won't calm down!" Jas shrieks. She slips away from Mom and pulls one of my curls until it nearly comes out. "You're a fake, Lily! Just like your hair! You hate all this? Huh? You're a liar!"

"Leave her hair alone! This instant!" Mom smacks Jasmine's hand and out falls one of my hair extensions. Not one of the permanent ones attached to my real hair, but an extra clip-in Mom had the hairstylist add tonight for drama. Mom shrieks.

Jas turns on Mom. "You're a traitor too! You let her take my job and now my boyfriend!"

"You were sick, Jas." I get up off the couch. "And Chase was never your boyfriend. You never even met him before I did."

"Because I was vomiting my guts out! You saw the perfect opportunity to make your move. Innocent little country girl my…" Jas lunges for me again.

Mom steps in between us and holds on to Jas.

"Let's sit down and discuss this in a civilized manner. Jasmine, you know it's good for the ad campaign for the public to believe Lily and Chase are dating. Get a grip."

"Are you blind, Mother? They really *are* dating!"

A little smile curves at the corner of Mom's lips. "Is that so?" She turns to face me. "When did this happen? And when were you going to share the news? Everyone sit down. We are not barbarians."

Jasmine sits on a chair next to the sofa and folds her arms in front of her. She seems to have moved from raging to pouting. I sit on the couch on the opposite side of Mom.

"Well, Lily?" Mom says.

I look at Jas. "I wanted to tell you. But I didn't want to hurt you. After the concert he sent me some beef jerky…"

Jas snorts.

"He asked me to meet him. We were hiding from the paparazzi…"

"And me." Jas closes her eyes and winces.

"I didn't mean to like him. I couldn't help it. And then I kept thinking maybe it would all go away. He's a pop star…I thought he probably would never want to see me again. I mean… he has to for the ad campaign, but I didn't see any reason to hurt you…"

"Hurt me?" Jas chokes. Her eyes are watery. "What do think you've done?"

Mom sits up tall. "Jasmine. A couple of posters in your room and some wishful thinking do not a boyfriend make. This is fantastic news."

"Oh my gosh!" Jas yells.

"Stop your antics." Mom clenches her teeth.

"Look!" Jas screams. "On…on…the balcony!"

We turn to look just as a black-clad photographer leaps down from our balcony to the one below. We run to the edge and see him scurry inside the dark apartment underneath ours and out of sight.

"Oh, no!" Mom wavers like she might faint. "What did he see? And hear? I've told you girls since you were…were…two! Control your behavior! We're ruined!"

Mom pushes us inside the flat and closes the French doors. "Did anyone get a good look at him? Was he French or English? Was he from the London Star? Hurry! Go into your room and close all the windows. I'm calling Interpol."

We go to our room, and Jas falls on her bed, burying her face in her pillow. I lie on my bed, staring up at the ceiling, my heart dropping with every sniffle I hear coming from Jas's side of the room.

Finally, Mom appears in the doorway. "I spoke to all my connections and hopefully, we can keep this under wraps. In the mean time, I expect perfect behavior. No more slip-ups."

"It's all Lily's fault!" Jas bolts upright, her voice ragged.

"My fault? You're the one who attacked *me*!"

Mom presses her fingers into her temples. "Jasmine—go to my room. You're sleeping with me

tonight. I'll have to separate the two of you like infants."
She takes a deep breath. "You girls have no idea what you
may have done."

Fifteen

"The perfume of a woman, it is her secrecy. To reveal, it is to strip itself in front of anybody." ~Louis Aragon

*R*oyale Perfume Princess a Fake! That's just one of the headlines, with a front page picture of Jasmine pulling out one of my hair extensions. Worse is the spread inside the newspaper. They somehow got my freshman yearbook picture, complete with short ponytail, no make-up, and braces. The caption reads: *Hya's Homely Daughter Steals the Spotlight.*

Mom had Curtis go to a newspaper stand early this morning and bring her all the tabloids. The worst one, for Mom at least, is a front page picture in the London Star of Mom smacking down Jas's arm when Jas was pulling my hair. Mom's eyes are wild with anger, and the headline reads: *Make-up Mogul Meltdown*. I think it could have been worse, like *Make-up Mogul Monster*, but nevertheless, Mom is devastated.

Big announcement: I feel sorry for Mom. For the first time ever. And especially because it's all my fault. If I would have just told Jasmine the truth from the beginning, this never would have happened. Sure, she would have been mad, but now multiply mad times three and add a double dose of betrayal. Now I'm the big ugly loser fake who stole my sister's career, Jas is the envious victim, and Mom, who has spent years perfecting her refined image, is now an unstable psychopath in need of anger management therapy.

After she read all the rags, Mom stayed in her room for over an hour and came out with red puffy eyes. Another reason I feel sorry for Mom: she never cries. Not even when she kissed me goodbye three years ago at the Houston airport, Dad waiting for me several feet away. Who leaves their twelve-year-old daughter behind to go start a new life and doesn't even cry about it? I didn't cry either. Not in front of her, and not in front of Dad. I didn't want him to think I was sad to stay with him. As soon as I got back to the ranch, I went for a fast gallop on Fire Star, and then I cried. I cried so hard I couldn't see a thing, but it didn't matter. Riding Fire Star is like flying an airplane on automatic pilot. She knows the way to our favorite spots, and she knows her way home, too.

I rode and cried like that for days, and that's when I realized how much I loved flowers—the one thing Mom and I have in common. Mom always had fresh flowers in every room of our house, for as long as I could remember.

After she left, Dad let the last bouquets die and wouldn't let our housekeeper throw them out. The water turned a greenish-brown and started to smell rancid. Everywhere you looked, there were wilted flowers, their heads bent down, just like Daddy's.

I guess the housekeeper couldn't take it anymore, because when I came home from school after one of her cleaning days, they had all vanished. The vases had been washed and stored away. As hard as it was to watch the flowers die and hang there all broken, it was worse to see them gone. I rode Fire Star into the prairie and started picking every last wildflower I could see, tears streaming down my face. Foxglove, Daisies, Goldenrod. I piled them so high I had to roll them up in the bottom of my shirt and ride back with one hand on the reigns. When I got home, I took all the vases back out and put wildflowers all over the house.

I'll never forget the look on Dad's face when he walked in the door, hung his hat on the peg in the foyer, and turned to see a vase full of fresh Texas blossoms on the entryway table. I held my breath. He looked at me, his tired eyes rimmed in red, yet smiling, even though they glistened wet. It was then I vowed to make Dad happy— and be as different from Mom as I could possibly be.

When Mom finally came out of her room she announced that the commercial shoot at the Eiffel Tower would go on as planned. "Keep calm and carry on," she said. Her favorite quote of all time. So off we went like nothing happened. Mom and I did, anyway. Jas refused to leave the flat, claiming her life was over. It must have been the headline, *Jealous Jasmine Goes for the Jugular*, that sent her over the edge.

So here I am in a white tent again, with three people working on my hair and make-up, and no Jas to coach me. I'm terrified that Chase won't show up. And terrified that he will. Now he knows I'm not really beautiful. That my hair is not really all mine. That underneath it all, I'm just a plain, homely, nothing special girl.

"Look up, Mademoiselle." One of the make-up artists brushes some finishing powder under my lower lashes. I feel a tear break through and run into the powder. She quickly blots it with a tissue. "Mademoiselle, it is not so bad. No one looks the same without their make-up. You are beautiful girl."

Even the make-up artist knows about the tabloids? I close my eyes and try to think of something—anything—else, but can't stop another tear from slipping through.

"We cannot do your make-up this way. I give you a moment?" The make-up artist puts down her brush and tells the others something in French about taking a short break.

Mom walks into the tent, her face like stone. I'm afraid she'll yell at me for not being ready, but she only sighs. "I've spoken with Mrs. Donovan. She's mortified, as we all are, but said Chase will go on with the ad campaign. I guess he has to, really. There's nothing in the contract about backing out because of a little bad press."

"I'm sorry, Mom."

"Stop being sorry, Lily, and start fixing things."

"How?" It comes out like a sob.

"Stop crying, and make the best commercial you're capable of." Mom walks out of the tent and orders the style team back in.

Taking a deep breath, I focus on the task at hand. I let this whole perfume thing happen to me, and now I have to take responsibility for it. Like it or not, I am the *Royale* Perfume Princess.

When the stylists finish, I walk toward the main staging area with Mom, determined to do this right. I've gone over the directions for the commercial dozens of times, even though there isn't much to it. There aren't any speaking lines, but I'm sure there's still plenty I could mess up.

Dozens of people are working behind the scenes, but Mom tells me to focus on the director, Milo Milenkovic, and do exactly what he says. "Remember, we have only one day to shoot this; there's no time for mistakes," she reminds me.

As we get closer, I see Chase. He's talking to the director when I walk up, and just looking at him from a distance takes my breath away. He looks so earnest, so sweet, like there isn't a bit of arrogance in him. He shakes Milo's hand and turns toward the set. Toward me. I stop. I can no longer move my feet. What does he think of me after reading the tabloids?

"Lily!" Milo gets to me first and kisses both my cheeks. His eyes run up and down me before focusing on my face. Spinning around, he yells at my make-up artist. "Monique! Too much. Tone this down immediately!"

Chase shoots me a sympathetic look. I give him a little wave, but then quickly look away. Monique sits me down in a folding canvas chair and I lower my lids so she can adjust my eye shadow with a soft brush. She mutters under her breath in French as she takes a tissue to the blush on my cheeks. Was she trying to compensate for my ugly picture in the tabloids this morning with an extra layer of make-up?

When I open my eyes, it's Chase I see, not Monique, who's now fiddling in her bag.

"Hey," Chase says. "You okay?"

I try to speak but can only nod my head. Monique pulls a pinkish beige lipstick from her huge black case and applies it to my mouth.

A man from the crew touches Chase on the arm. "Mr. Donovan, I need you to return to wardrobe. Please come with me."

"I'll be right back," Chase says to me as he is led toward a huge fabric screen. He walks sideways, his eyes lingering on mine until he disappears behind it.

"Let's get moving people!" An assistant directors shouts.

My pulse quickens. I need Jasmine, or at least to

remember everything she's taught me. I can hear her voice speaking to me: *it has to come from the inside, Lily.* In order to pull this off, I have to believe. But how can I believe now, after the whole world has seen the real me?

"Mademoiselle." The same man that led Chase away hands me a piece of paper, rolled like a little scroll, with a gold seal holding it closed. "Mr. Donovan asked me to give you this."

It's stationery from the Hotel de Crillon. I hold it in my hand like a treasure and close my eyes, afraid to open it. Slowly, I remove the seal and unroll the paper. It's a note from Chase, and a sonnet by William Shakespeare, in Chase's handwriting.

Lily,

I know how much you like Shakespeare, and this reminded me of you...

To gild refined gold, to paint the lily,
To throw a perfume on the violet,
To smooth the ice, or add another hue
Unto the rainbow, or with taper-light
To seek the beauteous eye of heaven to garnish,
Is wasteful and ridiculous excess.

(Lily, you're beautiful—nothing added.
Especially your heart.)

Holding the paper against my chest, I exhale and close my eyes.

To paint the Lily...

It's not the paint—not the perfume—not the clothes. Chase likes *me. Me!*

I have to smile, because deep down, I knew that already.

Sixteen

"The personality is to the man what the perfume is with the flowers." ~C.M. Schwab

"Take two!" Milo yells. Chase and I sit together in the sun on a cement ledge near *Le Palais de Challiot*, the Eiffel Tower looming in the background. We laugh and hold hands, then get up and run toward the Eiffel Tower. It's easy to laugh, because I feel a lightness I haven't felt in weeks, and because every few minutes Chase whispers something in my ear that makes me giggle.

"Excellent, Lily," Milo says to me after the fifth take. Do I have a knack for acting? But who's acting? I'm in love!

For the next scene, we move to the Eiffel Tower, and the commercial cuts to us running up the iron stairs of the Tower on our way to the top. On the first take, Chase trips on one of the steps and I have to catch him, which isn't easy to do with four-inch heels. Going up the stairs is grueling, even though we're really only going up and down the same flight over and over, pretending to be climbing to the top. My thighs ache. This sure beats the Stairmaster Mom makes Jas and I use every day in New York. We do the scenes several times, the director changing something every take until he's satisfied we can go on.

In our final scene, we overlook Paris from the Tower, and Chase holds me from behind. A fan blows my hair away from my face and I lean back in Chase's arms. They make me take my heels off so Chase is just the right height, a few inches taller than me. Milo says our feet won't show in this part of the commercial, anyway.

"Turn your faces a little more toward the camera this time, and let's try it again," Milo says. This is easy, and so fun! We don't have to say a word, just create a mood.

Even though we've been together all day, we haven't had a chance to really talk. The directors have been relentless, keeping us moving at a fast pace. "We're going to film some extra footage up here, in case we need it," the assistant director says. "Turn and face each other."

"Hey, you," Chase says when I turn and look at him. Does he have any idea how adorable he is?

"Hi," I say back.

The assistant director rolls his eyes and grunts.

Even that was too much talking for him. "Let's begin, please," he says. "Camera. Action."

After a few more takes, the director yells, "Cut!" Chase looks disappointed. "Why no kissing scenes?" he whispers.

"This is a perfume commercial," I tease. "Not a movie."

"I've seen kissing in commercials," Chase says in a serious voice.

"Yeah, I guess in those dumb jewelry commercials, where they try to brainwash people that diamonds somehow equal love." I've always hated those commercials, imagining some poor chap spending his last dime on some worthless heart necklace with a diamond so small you need a magnifying glass to see it, just because the commercial says it will make a woman love him. I'd rather have a handwritten sonnet from Shakespeare. Or a flower picked from a field.

"You don't like jewelry?"

"Not really," I admit.

"Good to know," he says. "Someone's birthday is coming up..."

"We need still shots from up here, and then that's a wrap," Milo tells everyone. "Lily, please turn back to your original position leaning against Chase."

I lean my back into Chase and feel his arms close in around me. He gives me a little extra squeeze before striking the correct pose. All I can think about is how happy I feel, except for the one teeny little thing nagging me—Jas. Alone. Sitting in our flat, missing it all, and probably crying.

We take a ton of still shots, and I remember all the poses Jas taught me. I close my eyes and see her posing at Lady Davignon's grungy photo shoot, so elegant and confident. Is it fair to Jas for me to be happy? To let myself like this? To like Chase? Is there room for two Laroche girls in Mom's world?

And what about Dad? It's bad enough that I filled in for Jas when she was sick, because I had to, but if he knew how much I'm enjoying this, would it break his heart?

When everything wraps up, Mom's beaming. I can tell I've pleased her. *Am I glad?*

Who *am* I?

Chase smiles at me and nothing else matters. His note. His sweetness. The silly goofy mistakes he made on the set. He took what started out as one of the worst days of my life and turned it into one of the best.

We take some more stills in front of a backdrop at the bottom of the Tower and then suddenly, it's all over. The crew starts to pack up their equipment. Mom takes Milo aside to talk business. Chase and I stand in the middle of everything like we don't know what to do next. Suddenly I feel shy. It's the first time we've been alone all day.

"Can I call you on Jas's phone later?" Chase sits down on one of the canvas chairs that hasn't been packed up yet. Has he really no clue?

Reality check. Jas. Tabloids. All is not well.

"Um…Jas is a little upset over the tabloids, so maybe it's not such a good idea."

"My mom told me you guys got zapped, but I didn't read it. I won't."

He didn't see it? "Then why did you give me that sonnet from Shakespeare?"

"Because my mom told me what happened, and I wanted you to know I think you're beautiful, just the way you are." He gets up from the chair and pulls me to him. "You're different." He pauses. "You're honest, and real."

Honest?

Real?

Two words I would *not* use to describe myself these days. My heart pounds.

"You never read the tabloids?" I ask. "I mean, I don't either—except for today. But you're in them, like, all the time."

"It's crazy. So many of your fans love you, but then a bunch of strangers decide to hate you. Make fun of you. If I didn't ignore it, it would hurt too much."

"Yeah," I said. "My Mom has a saying about that. Something about how people throw rocks at things they're jealous of."

"I'm not complaining," Chase says. "I know how lucky I am. I'm living my dream. Doing something I love. Not everybody has the chance to do that."

I can't help but think about Mom. She's doing what she loves, too. But once you have kids, you should put them first. I don't forgive her for a minute for leaving Texas. For leaving *me*.

"Do you still want to go out with me, Lily? Even with all the bad things, like the tabloids, that come with it?"

I hear him take a breath. How could he not know? How could he doubt?

"I do." It comes out hoarse. I wish I could tell him about Jas. Why I acted so strangely last night. Tell him everything. But I can't. Instead I put my head on his chest and memorize the feel of his shirt against my cheek, the sound of his heart. Neither one of us moves until we hear voices.

Chase takes a step back and lifts my hand above my head, then twirls me around like a ballerina. "Tonight, we celebrate!"

Tonight.

Jas.

How can I celebrate unless Jas is happy, too?

My only hope is that Jacques Davignon will be her viscount in shining armor. He's the only one who might be able to turn this whole thing around.

Seventeen

"Flattery, like perfume, should be smelled, not swallowed."
~Albanian Proverb

*J*as manages to look stunning, even after all that crying. She struts, on Jacques Davignon's arm, into *La Boehme* restaurant like she owns it. The restaurant—and Jacques, too. She's wearing a satiny silver cocktail dress and rhinestone heels. A small section of her hair is held back on each side with tiny diamond barrettes. She's not really speaking to me, but at least the storm has passed. Things can only get better, right?

When Jas got the news this afternoon that Jacques was still coming to dinner tonight, despite the tabloids, she was finally able to pull herself together. Mom called the Davignons and told them the entire scene was misconstrued, a complete falsehood. According to Mom, they told her they didn't believe a word of it, and of course Jacques would still accompany Jas to dinner.

I thought to myself, pictures don't lie. No matter what we tell people, forever more there will be evidence of Jas pulling my hair and of Mom screaming and batting her hand down. There are things you can't just sweep under the rug. I wish with all my heart that I could undo everything—push a rewind button and tell Jasmine the truth to begin with. Make things go back to the way they were.

"Just ignore the bad press and create some good," Mom told Jasmine after hanging up with the Davignons. "The public will forgive and forget."

Jas was silent, but she nodded her head and gave Mom a brave smile, giving me half a prayer that everything would be okay.

Watching her now with Jacques, I'm even more hopeful—except when I think about the stupid thing I did earlier. I left the note Chase gave me on the dresser when I went to take a shower. When I came back into our room, wrapped in a towel, Jas was reading it. She tossed it down, didn't even apologize for reading my stuff, and walked out.

I tug on the hem of my pale pink mini dress that keeps riding up, and check my appearance in the mirror in the foyer of the restaurant. My hair has been straightened and pulled back on one side in an asymmetrical sweep. Even though Chase says I don't need all these extras to look pretty, I still hope he likes how I look.

Mom's mood has steadily improved all day, and she beams as the maître d' escorts us to our table. Jas and Jacques sit on one end, and Mom and I sit on the other, making room for Chase and his entourage when they arrive.

"Jacques." Mom smoothes her napkin on her lap. "We would like to invite you to Lily's birthday party next week in New York. I know it's short notice—"

"Oh, please come!" Jas puts her arm through his. "Will you be my date?"

Mom is usually appalled at such straightforwardness, but coming from Jas, it seems normal. Jas has always been a flirt. Most guys know she could easily replace them, so she never seems desperate, but tonight she's different. Like the confidence she's always had is now only on the surface. She seems vulnerable to me.

Before Jacques can answer, we hear a commotion. Chase. His arrival anywhere is always chaotic. Jacques looks annoyed, and I have a feeling his sense of French decorum is being stretched to its limits. He sighs. "Thank you for the invitation, Madame Laroche, but I'm afraid I will be unable to attend."

Jas's eyes are round and scared. Her face falls with all the sadness of child whose ice-cream cone has just hit the sidewalk.

Before anyone else can speak, our faces are lit up by a giant flash. Someone has taken a picture. Another flash. Then another. I turn to see the maître d' and a cook drag away a man with a camera, just as Chase approaches the table. Jacques's lips are pursed tightly together. Jas unwinds her arm from Jacques and leans toward Chase so he can kiss her cheek.

I want Chase to know how happy I am to see him, so I start to stand up and go to him, but Mom pushes me back in my chair. I know the rules—women don't rise to greet men—but I feel like I have a lot of making up to do. Chase shakes Jacques's hand, kisses Mom, and then finally gets to me. He kisses me on the cheek, but so close to my mouth that his lips touch the corner of mine. I can barely breathe.

Chase sits down next to me and grabs my hand, and this time I don't try to pull away. I'm still embarrassed in front of Jas, but I don't want to hurt Chase either. Luckily, the tabloids never accurately reported what Jas and I were fighting about. Most of the articles said the fight was about me taking over the Laroche Empire, so Jas's crush on Chase is still a secret. She was made out to be the victim, and I the villain—the ugly duckling sister who stole Jasmine's job. I'm so glad Chase doesn't read the tabloids.

Dinner is awkward. No one dares talk about the newspapers, so the conversation revolves around the Eiffel Tower shoot, which leaves Jasmine looking pained. She's been in a funk since Jacques said he can't go to my Sweet Sixteen, and he's been moody, too, ever since Chase arrived. I'm starting to wonder if they'll ever make it as a couple. Who was I kidding? They live on separate continents. I slump down in my chair as the bill is paid, my hope disappearing with every glance at Jas.

"As promised," Mom announces to the table, "we'll take a stroll in Montmartre, and then a river cruise." She sounds like a tour guide.

Chase's mom claps her hands together like a child. "That sounds wonderful, Hya. I've always wanted to see *Sacré-Coeur*."

We leave the restaurant in two cars and get out near *Place du Tertre*, so we can walk like good Parisians, the only difference being we are followed everywhere we go. I decide to ignore everything: Mom, Jas, the paparazzi, the body guards. Everything but Chase. If I make believe hard enough, I can pretend it's just the two of us.

We walk hand in hand, taking in all the sights. Lights twinkle everywhere. There's so much beauty in Paris, when you choose to see it. Chase made me fall in love with New York for the first time, and now he's sprinkled his magic dust on the City of Light. *Vive la France!*

Chase and his mom seem to be fascinated by everything they see, and repeatedly stop in their tracks. I take a peek at Jas. She doesn't even perk up when we walk by one of her favorite boutiques, or ask to go inside. I've never seen her like this. Not even interested in a little retail therapy? My heart sinks; she and Jacques aren't even holding hands anymore.

We approach one of the most tourist-y places in

all of Paris. So beneath Mom, but she seems pleased to show it to Mrs. Donovan. Artist easels and displays are everywhere, enticing passersby to get their portraits done. After walking past several, we stop. There, front and center, is a drawing of Chase, surrounded by drawings of a few other celebrities.

"I thought you've never been here before," I tease. "Evidence," I say, pointing at his image.

Chase laughs. "Let's get our portrait done, Lily. You and me together." Chase smiles at me, his eyes pleading.

I glance at Mom. For all I know, this is against the rules, but she nods her head.

We choose an artist who has some really nice portraits on display, and ask him to do ours. He sits us together on a chair. He's so excited, I have no idea how he'll be able to hold his charcoal.

"Don't smile so big, Mademoiselle," he tells me. I giggle. "Do not move, *s'il vous plait*." He shakes his head.

I could sit in this chair forever, squeezed up next to Chase. The artist stares intently at our faces, working feverishly. I'm surprised how quickly he finishes the drawing, and even more surprised when I see it. I've seen myself in the mirror every day since my "transformation," but somehow seeing me in the sketch is different. It doesn't look anything like me. In the drawing I see a girl I don't recognize, sitting next to Chase Donovan, like she belongs there.

"Well, he got you down right," I say. "But that

sure doesn't look like me."

Chase cups my chin in his hand. "What do you mean? It looks *exactly* like you."

Everyone murmurs about what a good job the artist has done and how much it looks like both of us. Quite a crowd has gathered—normal for Chase, but not for me. I've never liked being the center of attention, and I've done a good job keeping myself out of it for nearly sixteen years. But tonight, I have to admit, I don't mind so much. I feel pretty… and… special? Like maybe it's okay for me to shine, too?

The artist slips the drawing into a stiff plastic sleeve backed with cardboard and gives it to Chase. "It's free," he says with a strong French accent.

"Please, Monsieur." Chase tries to pay the artist, but he shakes his head.

"*Gratuit. Free,*" he insists.

"*Merci Beaucoup,*" Chase tells him and shakes his hand. I see Chase slip some bills to one of his body guards and tell him to give the man a tip once we've gone away.

"For you," Chase says, handing the portrait to me. "I hope you like it."

"I love it." I look in Chase's eyes. It feels like I really said, I love *you*. I gulp.

Out of the corner of my eye, I spot Jasmine. She doesn't look happy—at all. She pretends to examine some paintings at a nearby booth, and I notice she's alone, no Jacques, no paparazzi, no body guard. Except for her dazzling attire, she could be any tourist plucking her way through the *Place du Tertre*.

We start to move on. "I'll be right back," I tell Chase.

I slide up next to Jas and tap her on the shoulder. "Hey."

"What do you want?" She doesn't look at me.

"Where's Jacques?" I try to keep my voice light.

"Why do you care?"

"Please Jas... I do care."

"He left." Jas takes a deep breath. "Something about a 'prior engagement.' We all know what that means." She covers her face with her hands and then drops them, turning to face me. "Go back to your boyfriend, Lily. I'm happy for you—really I am." She turns away. "Just go. Please."

I walk back to Chase with a heavy heart.

Eighteen

"Truths and roses have thorns about them."

~Henry David Thoreau

On the Seine river cruise, Chase and I sit together on the farthest seat in the boat. There are three rows, and Mom, Mrs. Donovan, and Jas are seated in the front, leaving the middle row for the two body guards who came on board with us. With that small degree of separation, I do my best to imagine Chase and I are alone.

I haven't cruised the Seine since I was at least ten, but I know all the sights by heart. If there's one thing Mom did do right, it was to teach us about culture and history. I stare up at the illuminated steeple of Notre Dame and imagine what it was like to live in the thirteenth century. The detail of the cathedral is mind boggling. It's like I'm seeing everything for the first time, through Chase's eyes.

As we get close to *La Conciergerie*, all lit up in its stunning glory, I tell Chase the story of how it started out as a royal castle, but then was turned into a prison for five hundred years.

"It's so beautiful," Chase says. "How could they use it as prison?"

I rest my head on his shoulder. "During the French Revolution, it housed aristocrats waiting for the guillotine, including Marie Antoinette."

Chase asks me lots of questions. He doesn't stop holding my hand—or smiling.

As much as I try to pretend Jas isn't sitting two rows up, I can't help but look at the back of her head. She turns to the side and looks toward the shore. A soft summer breeze blows her hair back, and I see her brush away a tear.

How can I ever really be happy knowing she's so sad?

"Everything's so amazing, here," Chase says, squeezing my hand. The stark contrast between the happy tone of his voice and Jas's tears unsettles me.

The boat slowly winds its way down the dark brown water of the Seine, the sky growing darker and darker as the cityscape quickly peppers with light.

As we approach the Grenelle Bridge by the *Île des Cygnes*, I suddenly see her. Lady Liberty, in miniature. I'd forgotten that Paris had its own smaller replica. The lighted Eiffel Tower glows in the background, not far away.

"Look!" Chase exclaims. "It's a little Statue of Liberty! How cool!" He puts his arm around my shoulders. "Just like our first date!"

We quickly approach her, and I stare at her face. Her giant American counterpart seemed to be telling me to stand up to Mom and Jas, to go ahead and follow my heart with Chase. But now this evil mini version is shouting at me that blood is thicker than water. That Jas is more important.

What do you stand for? Liberty or Loyalty? She's your sister…

But she never even went out with him! Not once! And even if I stop seeing Chase, it's not like Jas will have him anyway. And what about his feelings?

It's like she says back to me… *but at least you won't either. And Chase can have any girl in the world. He could replace you by tomorrow. But you can never replace your sister.*

The boat lurches, and Chase tightens his arm around me. Clouds, noticeable even in the increasingly dark sky, cover half the moon and most of the stars. We come to a stop near a bridge where Mom has arranged for the drivers to pick us up instead of returning to the place we left from, and we all disembark. Jas gets off first, ignoring everyone, and walks directly to the street above.

We've landed in one of my favorite areas of Paris. Antique booksellers line the river with rows of rare books and engravings, mixed in with a few pieces of art and some Parisian souvenirs. I momentarily forget about breaking up with Chase. There's music, too, and I can't wait to show him. I grab his hand and lead him to the street.

"Can we stay here awhile?" I ask the group. "I want to look through some books."

Jas groans and rolls her eyes. She's never been interested in books, or antiques, for that matter. "It looks like it might rain soon, and these shoes are killing me. I'm going back to the flat."

"Betty?" Mom asks. "What would you like to do?"

"If it's all right with you, Hya, I'd love to look around for a while. It's so quaint."

"It's settled then. One of the drivers can take Jas to the flat while we browse, and then come back to take you and Chase to your hotel." Mom kisses Jas on both cheeks. "See you later, darling."

Jas gives everyone an air kiss. "Are any of the body guards coming with me?" She looks at Mom expectantly.

"I hardly think that's necessary, but... Jean Claude, go with Jasmine, si'l vous plait."

Jasmine grimaces and shakes her head. Mom just doesn't get it. Why does she continually embarrass Jas by drawing attention to her seeming fall from celebrity? Jas pulls her sunglasses out of her purse and puts them on, even though it's dark outside. How can she see a thing? Is she trying to hide her eyes from us?

"Bye, Jas!" I call as she gets in the car and Jean Claude shuts the door behind her. She has to forgive me, right? I'm her *only* sibling, after all. When the car pulls away and Jas is gone, a sense of freedom hits me. I have an hour, maybe two, left in Paris with Chase, and I'm going to enjoy every second. "How much time do we have, Mom?" I grab Chase's hand and get ready to move.

"Let's meet back here in one hour. That should give everyone plenty of time." Mom's voice is pleasant, but I know she could care less about the books, too. It reminds me of another one of Mom's rules: when entertaining guests, think of activities that *they* would enjoy, not necessarily what you would prefer. I guess it's her way of putting others first, even though I always thought she did it to impress people and make them like her. Whatever her motives, tonight I'm glad for the rule.

"We're down to two bodyguards and your American driver," Betty says nervously. "Should we stick together until Jean Claude returns?"

Chase pats the arm of his main bodyguard. "We'll be fine with just T. J." He puts his arm around his mom and squeezes her, then leans down and kisses her cheek. "Love you, Mom. Bye!" He grabs my hand and turns to go.

"Hold it." Betty laughs. She looks at Mom. "Can your driver walk with us and let the kids have the two bodyguards?"

"Fabulous idea!" Mom smiles.

"See ya!" Chase says this time without pausing, and pulls me down the street.

"You might need an umbrella!" Betty calls after

us.

"We're fine, Mom!" Chase is almost running.

We pass the first few displays in an attempt to put distance between our mothers and us. I giggle and keep up with him despite my high heels and a blister. The ground is damp and we have to step around a few puddles, so I don't dare go barefoot, but my feet are killing me.

"I could sure use my old pair of cowboy boots about now," I say laughing.

Chase looks down at my shoes. "Those have to hurt. I wish I could trade you, but I think my feet are bigger. Maybe."

"Hey!" I laugh. "Well, too bad, because these would look great on you! Don't worry, I'm perfectly fine."

I'm not really. I probably won't even be able to walk tomorrow, but who cares, I'll be on a plane for almost eight hours.

"Wow. Look at these." Chase drags me over to a display of ancient sheet music.

"Those are original, handwritten works by Jean Pierre Duval," the woman attendant explains in a heavy French accent. "Written in 1682. Are you a musician young man?"

Chase squeezes my hand, and I giggle.

"I love music," Chase says to her sincerely. He examines the notes intensely. "I'm not familiar with Duval, but these are beautiful."

I love the fact she has no idea who we are—and I

can tell Chase does, too. She shows us all her sheet music, and a tiny violin she claims was used by Mozart when he lived in Paris in the late seventeen hundreds. Chase turns it carefully in his hands when she lets him hold it, his eyes all lit up. He glances over at me. "Isn't this cool? To think Mozart played his music with this very violin."

I'm not sure I believe her, but I guess it's possible. "I didn't know you liked classical music," I say.

"My father's a concert pianist." Chase looks down at an old album cover. "I grew up listening to classical music."

"Where is he now? Does he ever travel with you?"

"Sure, all the time. They just thought with your mom all alone and everything, it would be more comfortable for her to just hang out with my mom without all that couple stuff. You know."

I know exactly what he means. When Jas was hanging all over Jacques, I didn't mind holding hands with Chase in front of her nearly as much. But when she was all alone next to us it felt awkward. "That was so sweet of your parents... so thoughtful."

"It's okay. They're together like twenty-four-seven, every day of the year. They probably could use a break."

Vaguely, I remember what it was like to be a whole family. "That must be nice... them being together so much."

"It is." Chase stops. "I mean... sorry. About your family." He gives me this sad, almost pitying look.

"It's okay. I'm used to it. I guess." We start walking again. "No, that's not really true. I like living in Texas with my dad, but I never get used to not having my sister… or a mom."

Chase tightens his arm around my shoulder. "How did it happen that you and Jas ended up living apart?"

"When our parents got divorced, Mom moved permanently to New York. Jas wanted to go with her, but I'd always been closer to my dad. I couldn't leave him, you know, all alone in Texas."

Chase's eyes look sad. I have to look away so I don't cry.

"That must've been hard," he says. "To choose."

"It wasn't so hard to choose between Mom and Dad. The hard part was Jas. Before… they… left…" My throat feels like it's closing up. "We were really close."

Chase leads me to a bench and we sit down, the street light above shining on his wavy hair. "That picture of my sister. The one you saw in my dressing room that night?" Chase pushes his hair out of his eyes. "The reason I always carry it with me…" He pauses. "We were really close, too. She died. In a car accident, a little over two years ago. She was only seventeen."

I squeeze my eyes shut, but I feel them fill up anyhow. I take Chase's hand, but I can't find any words.

"The worst part is… I hardly spent any time with her the whole year before she died. I was always on the road, and she was in school. She was going to spend the whole summer on the tour bus with me..." Chase's voice cracks. "But then... on the last day of school..."

"I'm so sorry," I whisper. I remember the words I said to him on the Hudson River, *who carries a picture of their sister around?* I cringe.

"Just don't let what happened between your mom and dad keep you and Jas apart, Lily. There's nothing like a sister or brother."

I give him a big hug. "I'm so sorry," I say again.

"It's okay. We try and remember the good times. She was one of the happiest people I've ever known. Mom likes to say Jess closed her eyes that day on earth, and opened them in heaven. She's always with me. Here." He touches his chest. "Keeping me grounded. Reminding me what's important in life."

Chase gets to his feet and holds his hand out to me. "Come on, let's see if we can find some old Shakespeare around here."

We walk hand in hand to the next booth that's filled with old books, and Chase helps me look for ones in English. "Do you have any Shakespeare?" he asks the gentleman manning the booth. The man shakes his head.

"No wonder we make such a good couple," Chase says. "You like classical literature, and I like classical music—"

"Monsieur, you are that singer, no?" The man stares at Chase, and then me. "And you are one of those Laroche girls, no? The mean one?"

I still haven't figured out how Jas gets caught

pulling my hair—but I'm the mean one. "I...I'm not mea—"

"You must be confusing us with someone else." Chase pulls me along and then nods his head at T.J. who is walking several steps behind us like he's never seen us before. Maybe it's because I already know him, but if you ask me, he *looks* like a bodyguard—and he *looks* like he's following us. The French bodyguard is even more obvious in his black trench coat, in the middle of summer, complete with an earpiece and an antennae sticking out of one pocket.

"Come on," Chase says. "I don't want the rest of our evening spoiled."

I think to myself that it's already spoiled. I *am* the mean one. The one who broke the sister code. The one who stole her sister's whole entire life. And now, how do I fix it without breaking up with the world's sweetest boyfriend?

"Speaking of spoiling an evening," I say. "It's starting to rain." A large raindrop hits my arm at the same time I see Mom and Betty scurrying toward us.

"Here they come," Chase says. "Let's stand under this canopy."

"Both cars are back," Mom says breathlessly. "Time to call it a night." She gets as far under the canopy as she can. She hates the rain. "We're going to the car," she announces, and then leans in close to me. "Lily—you've got five minutes."

We watch as our moms run to the cars—well as

close to running as they can get in their high-heels—and then hug goodbye. They get into separate cars to wait for us. My heart sinks. I know what I have to do. I have to break up with him. Tonight. It's the only chance I'll have to do it in person, and spare him from coming to my birthday party. It's the right thing to do.

"Well, they're getting along great!" Chase pulls me in to face him.

The couple whose canopy we're standing under are attempting to close down their booth. "*Pardon,*" the man says and shoos us away.

Despite the rain, we walk slowly toward the cars. I have to tell him now, face to face. It's the least I can do. I grab Chase's arm underneath a streetlamp and turn to face him, but then look down at my feet. "Wait. I... uh... there's something I need to tell you."

"You look so serious. What's wrong?" Chase pulls me close to him and I turn my head to rest against his chest. I take a deep breath, wanting to memorize his smell. The clean mix of soap, rain, and Mom's *Royale pour homme.* He's worn it every time I've seen him.

"Chase... I..." Closing my eyes, I exhale. The rain begins to fall harder. I picture Jas, sad, defeated. *I need to do this.*

"Chase, I... I can't see you anymore. And I can't do any more perfume ads."

"Lily, what's wrong?" Chase grabs both my hands in his. "Is it the paparazzi?"

I think about making it easier and saying yes. I

can't tell him Jas's secret and betray her more than I already have, but I can't lie anymore either.

I close my eyes and take a deep breath. "If I'm with you… I hurt someone else. Someone important to me. I can't tell you any more than that."

"Who, Lily?"

"Chase. Please don't. This is not what I *want*; it's what has to be."

"Can you explain that, Lily? You're not making any sense."

"Jas will take over the perfume ads."

"Who cares about the perfume ads! Why are you doing this?"

"Chase, I'm sorry." I pull my hands away from his and leave him standing alone on the sidewalk, pelted by the rain. Turning to look at him, my heart breaks and I run back to hug him one last time. "You're the best thing that ever happened to me," I choke out.

Chase says nothing, leaving his arms against his sides, like a statue.

Nineteen

"Two things make the women unforgettable, their tears and their perfume." ~Sacha Guitry

I turn and run to the car and climb in next to Mom.

"You're soaking wet! I'm sure you've ruined that dress—and those shoes." Mom's tone is only mildly chastising. She chatters on without stopping. "The two of you make such an adorable pair. I'll have the best photographers take pictures at your party to release to the press. I mentioned to Chase's mother this evening, that he should come dressed as a prince."

I let her drone on, not bothering to tell her that Chase won't be at the party, or that my career with Laroche cosmetics has reached its end. There's been enough bravery for one day. One day that has turned out to be both the best and the worst day of my life.

I hold myself together all the way back to the flat. The rain pelts against the windshield making the bright lights of Paris seem like a blur. The streets are nearly empty now, and we're home in no time. We enter the building peacefully, no paparazzi in sight, and walk up the several flights of stairs to our floor.

"Take that dress off immediately," Mom says as we enter the flat. "We'll probably have to throw it away, but since you were photographed in it multiple times this evening, you probably shouldn't wear it again anyway." She tosses her handbag on the entryway table and walks toward her room.

Is everything disposable to her? First Dad and me, and now Jas?

"Sweet dreams, darling." Mom blows me a kiss goodnight. "I'm very proud of you," she whispers before closing the door to her room.

Her words hang in the air like dirty garments on a clothesline, meant to hold clean. I've never heard Mom say those words to me. *I'm proud of you.* Not once in all the years I brought home straight A report cards. Not when I won the county-wide poetry contest in fifth grade—or when I was accepted into the National Honor Society in ninth. Not for anything I've ever done.

I can barely breathe. The weight of Mom's words, mixed with what I've done to Chase, crush my chest and I stumble to the wall by the door of our bedroom. I can't let them hear me break down. I put my head against the wall and hold back a sob.

Slowly, I open the door and tiptoe into our room, careful not to wake Jas. Wiggling out of my wet dress, I let it fall to the ground in a heap. As I put on my pajamas, Jas stirs in her bed, and my heart stops. The pressure to break down is unbearable, but there's nowhere to go and cry. I tiptoe back out of the room and go to the couch. Curling up into the corner, I bury my head in one of Mom's silk pillows.

I want to sob—to scream—but I can't. I would never wake them up. Robotically, I get up and go into the kitchen to grab a dishtowel to protect Mom's pillow, and then go back to the couch and cry into the towel, muffling the sound, until I can cry no more. I cry over the mess I've made of everyone's life, including my own. I cry for Chase's sister Jess, for him, for his mom, and for his dad that I don't even know.

When I'm done crying, I look out into the darkness. There's just enough light coming in through the balcony doors from the moon and the stars, now that the rain has emptied the sky of its cover. I walk over to the television to grab the remote control. I almost never watch TV, but there's no point in trying to sleep now. I'll be better off sleeping on the airplane tomorrow and easing my way back into the New York time zone.

On the bookshelf surrounding the television, I sift through the row of black cases that contain the videos from our trips to France when Jas and I were little. I randomly pick one from the middle and place it in the

DVD player, grab the remote and the silk throw off the wing chair, and go sit back down on the couch. I press play.

The first thing that comes on the screen is Jas. She must have been about three. Beautiful, even as a child. She's sitting on Dad's lap while he pretends to tickle her. I laugh, remembering how Jas hated to be tickled, and Daddy could only pretend to do it, so she wouldn't cry. When it came to me, he could tickle me as hard as he wanted to. We'd even wrestle on the ground. But not Jas. She was always a princess.

The video switches to me, almost a toddler, sitting on the floor in Meme's old kitchen. I'm wearing a white cotton sundress and a headband with a giant white bow on my head. I'm hitting the ground with my hands, and whoever is taking the video is cooing to me. *Mom.* I swallow hard. I don't remember her paying that much attention to me. Ever. In the video, I grab the headband, pull it off, and throw it to the ground with a squeal. Then there's a break in the filming. Back on. The video *and* the headband. Mom's singing a childhood song to me in French to get my attention.

I don't know how many videos I watch, mesmerized. Jas and I on the beach in the South of France. The two of us feeding Meme's goats. Playing dress up. Jas dressed as a princess having tea parties, sometimes with me, and sometimes alone. Me riding a pony. The two of us running up the steps of a famous castle in the Loire Valley holding hands.

When I see the moon starting to fade and the beginning of dawn appearing in the sky from the balcony, I go to bed and wait for Mom to wake me.

Twenty

"The memory is the perfume of the heart."~George Sand

hunderstorms threaten to prevent us from landing at LaGuardia Airport. Normally, I'd be terrified, but I can't seem to care about anything. The pilot is given clearance and down we go, the turbulence making my stomach drop. It's a terrible sensation, similar to how my heart feels. I understand now why people use the word heartache. You really do feel it—the pain—in your heart.

The only thing on my mind is Chase. Chase standing in the rain. Arms at his side. The look of disbelief.

The rain has followed me all the way from Paris to New York and beats on the tiny airplane window. Jas sits next to Mom, across the aisle from me, looking a little green. Her and her sensitive stomach. The ruin of us all.

The wheels of the airplane touch down, hitting the ground in several bounces. There's a collective sigh of relief.

"Home," Jas says to Mom.

Where is home? Certainly not here for me. But Texas, and Fire Star, and even Dad seem like a faraway dream. Like I belong neither here nor there.

A Laroche Cosmetics company driver picks us up. Curtis helps us into the town car, and then leaves to hail himself a cab. As I settle in next to Mom, I have no idea where I'll ever find the courage to tell her I broke up with Chase. Or that I'm quitting the perfume campaign.

Mom looks at her agenda. "Five days until the party. So much to do."

I don't understand what the big deal is. It seems like she doesn't have to *do* anything—she has people doing everything for her.

She wrinkles her forehead. "And don't think of this as time off. I've hired Rocco D'Silva to give you some modeling lessons on Tuesday. Then on Wednesday there's a meeting at Laroche Cosmetics to plan the next *Royale* perfume commercial that you must attend, and a full day salon appointment on Thursday."

"Huh?" I shake my head in disbelief.

"Do you think those eyebrows will maintain themselves on their own?" Mom shifts in her seat. "And those hair extensions? They need to be redone. Manicure, pedicure, facial. Need I go on?"

"Why does she need Rocco D' Silva? She's doing

fine." Jas finally breaks her silence. *To defend me.*

"Who's Rocco D'Silva?" I ask. "And why do I need lessons?"

"A model needs to know how to move her body," Mom says snidely. "Jas has gotten you through, but some professional lessons will be good for you. How to pivot. Walk a runway. How to sit properly, for goodness sake."

Mom looks down at my legs, and I quickly cross my ankles. Now might be a good time to tell her the lessons won't be necessary. That I quit. As soon as Dad gets here for my party, her reign over my life is over. I've got it all planned out. I'm going back with him, no matter what she says.

"And we'll need to make you a portfolio and some composite cards."

I see Jas shake her head before looking out her window. Even she seems to have had enough of Mom. I think about standing up for both of us, but what's the point? There's no way to beat Mom. Except to get out of Dodge.

When we get back to the apartment, the doormen take up our bags, and I go straight to my room. I'm already lying on my bed when suddenly Mom yells at me through the intercom. "Lily, come down here immediately!"

I go downstairs to find Mom standing over one of my suitcases. Ingrid is sorting through my dirty clothes, holding a Hermes scarf with a big oily mark in the middle. The scent of my own perfume wafts through the air. I haven't used it since the day I got to New York. I only keep it with me to remind me of home. Of Texas. I brace myself.

"What's the meaning of this?" Mom has her hands on her hips, eyes flashing. "Whose is it? Dior? Cartier?"

"What are you talking about?" Maybe if I play dumb…

"This perfume!" Mom snatches the scarf from Ingrid's hands and shoves it near my nose. "If anyone finds out you use another designer's perfume, the press will have a heyday. Who makes it?"

When I stand there with my mouth wide open, thinking up any answer other than the truth, Mom begins rifling through my suitcase. I swallow hard as I see her reach for the tiny white plastic vial, empty, with the top missing. Busted. She puts it to her nose. I hold my breath. How could I be so careless?

"It's mine." I'm not sure she hears me.

"Yours?" Mom smells it again.

I feel a hand on my shoulder. It's Jas. "What's going on?" She sniffs the air.

Mom passes her the Hermes scarf. "It seems we have a budding perfume designer on our hands."

Jas takes a whiff. "Smells good." She looks at me. "You made this?"

I nod my head. I can't look at Mom. I can already imagine the smirk on her face.

Twenty-one

"Dignity is like a perfume; those who use it are scarcely conscious of it." ~Christina of Sweden

Rocco D'Silva stands looking at me, hands on his hips. "The girl has no rhythm," he says to who knows who. We're alone on a runway stage, with music playing in the background. Music that was supposed to loosen me up. Thank goodness Mom had other things to do and isn't witness to another round of my incompetency.

"Rocco's the best in the business," she said on the way to drop me off. Like I was supposed to be impressed. I didn't answer.

Then she changed the subject. "Why didn't you tell me you're making perfume? I could have helped you.

It's my business you know. *Our* business."

Exactly, I thought. Did she need it spelled out after all these years? Have I not made it perfectly clear I want nothing to do with Laroche Cosmetics?

Obviously there is no obvious with Mom. Exhibit A: I'm standing on a runway taking modeling lessons I do not want, for a career I do not want.

"Remember to stay in the box," Rocco says, speaking of the masking tape square on the floor. "Think of it as a frame, Lily. And you are a live photograph. Remember the camera."

I swing my hips, twirl, and move from side to side like he demonstrates, remembering to pause after every move for the imaginary click of the camera. Totally embarrassing.

"Shoulders back. You're slouching again. Move. Pause. Move. Pause." Rocco claps his hands together twice, like he wants me to speed it up. "Try something different with your arms, like this." He cocks his head and puts one hand up against his ear, elbow in the air, pauses, then turns and pretends to flip imaginary long hair. He pauses again, then lifts one arm above his head, and puts the other on his hip, like a flamenco dancer. I do my best to imitate him, hating every minute.

Without Chase, this isn't fun anymore.

"Let's move on to runway," Rocco finally says. Would it kill him to mask some of the exasperation?

"I want you to pretend there's an imaginary line running down the middle of the stage, like a tightrope, and it's your job to stay on it. I want you to walk, leaning back, one foot in front of the other, like this." Rocco struts down the catwalk. "Toes pointing out slightly, hips swinging, both feet on the line."

He looks exactly like a runway model. Or at least moves like one. I try his technique, one foot directly in front of the other, imagining the tight rope. I wobble.

"Toes out. That will give you balance. Shoulders way back. Swing your hips." He demonstrates again.

I turn my toes out and start over. Down the runway I go.

"Not so much. You look like a penguin. Toes *slightly* out."

There are so many things to think of at once, I'm not sure I can do them all at the same time. I try again. And again. It gets a little easier each time. It's weird, walking like this feels arrogant, but at the same time it's impossible to walk like this and not feel confident. It kind of feels good. Better than slouching along, I have to admit.

"This is the way you should walk everywhere, Lily. Down the sidewalk, when you enter a room, anywhere you go."

I imagine myself walking down the hallways at school like this. It would look ridiculous. Even the most popular beauty queens, and there are plenty in Texas, don't lay it on this thick. But I'm intrigued that there's a science to it. An actual way to walk that makes you look and feel like something special.

"Better. Much better." Rocco nods his head in

approval. "You look like a new girl."

I feel like a new girl. I like how it feels to stand up straight, and walk like you have a purpose. I get to the end of the runway, turn, and do it again.

Where have I seen this before? I picture Mom's book, *Any Woman can be Beautiful: The French Way to Fabulous.* Some chapter toward the end. I remember a diagram on how to walk—that I'd quickly skipped over.

I'll never forget the day the book arrived at the ranch, about a year after Mom and Jas left. Mom sent me a copy in a pretty package. She signed it, *To my darling, Lily. Continue to blossom, my little flower. Love always, Mom.* Gag. I think I threw it across the room. But I've looked at it from time to time, when I can't help myself. Somewhere in all the garbage about how to look and act like a model even if you aren't one, she teaches the proper way for a lady to walk.

I think about Daddy. He has his own proud walk, almost like a cowboy. I guess I'm the only one in the family who walks like a worm. And worms don't even walk, they crawl. I have zero interest in doing runway work. I refuse. But I decide I can change my walk. Just a little.

"Now this time when you reach the end of the runway, I want you to pivot." Rocco struts down the runway again, and this time pauses at the end, posing for a make-believe audience. He pushes one hip out at an angle, pauses, and then pivots. He turns his head to look one more time at the "audience" and then struts back down the runway. "Go!" he instructs me. "Swing those hips!"

I dutifully perform the move, knowing I'll never have reason to use it. Maybe I'll stop slouching, and maybe I'll try to walk better, but I know in my heart that modeling is not for me. I have to tell Mom. Again. In a way that will make her listen.

Twenty-two

"A good name is better than a good perfume."

~Ethiopian Proverb

We take the elevator to the top floor of Laroche Cosmetics. No matter how many times I'm dragged to Mom's Empire, the view of New York City from the floor to ceiling windows takes my breath away. Even a country girl can appreciate the looming skyscrapers and staggered buildings, like a large bouquet of gray concrete. Pretty in its own way.

Mom walks past the receptionists' desk at a fast clip. "Good morning, ladies."

"Good Morning, Madame," the three receptionists say unison. Then to me, "Good morning, Miss Laroche."

"Morning," I say, barely slowing down. I want to

say, *it's Carter. My last name's Carter!* But I just smile instead. Jasmine decided long ago to hyphenate her name to Laroche-Carter, so I guess they figured I had done the same.

I peek inside my Louis to make sure it's still in there. My plan. Even I wouldn't quit on Mom without finding a way to ease Jas back into the perfume campaign. All I need is a few minutes alone with Mom's producer. If he likes it, he can present it to Mom, and presto! Jas will be back in business.

Inside the board room, I sit quietly next to Mom as she orders her staff around. I run my finger along the edge of the polished wood table, only half listening to the conversation. It seems she's changed her mind about the next location.

"The Eiffel Tower was cliché, but necessary." Mom taps her pen against the table. "The official symbol of France for the *masses*."

That's how Mom insults the people who buy her perfume. She calls them *the masses*. Before I remember that I won't even *be* in the next shoot, I blurt out, "How about Texas?"

The entire room stares at me. I'm terrified Mom will humiliate me in front of everyone. *Texas? Never!*

"We'll save that for the *new perfume*, Lily," Mom says in an even tone. "*Royale* is elegance. Romance. International flair. The essence of royalty." She glances around the room, one hand gesturing in the air. "Think castles. Fairy tales."

All I can think about are the words *new perfume*. Does she mean mine? My unnamed, homemade, Texas-style perfume?

Names of castles and romantic international landmarks are thrown out. Fountains in Italy, a hilltop in Greece. Someone suggests the Taj Mahal, and Mom shoots it down immediately. "We're talking about Lily and Chase, here. Think youthful. The Taj Mahal is completely inappropriate. We want fun—not everlasting, marital love."

What would Mom know about that?

"We'll resume this later," Mom says, looking at her watch. "I want everyone back here in exactly one hour—with the perfect locale. I've got other business to attend to."

The room clears, and only Mom and I are left. She gathers her things. "Come with me to the laboratory."

Mom has a small laboratory adjacent to her office where she works on creating her own perfumes before sending the formulas to be developed in the factory. Beautiful glass shelves are lined with tiny blue bottles. That's one thing I do admire about Mom. Even after all her success, she still hasn't passed this part of the business to hired perfume designers. She does it herself. It's her passion. It's maybe the one thing I get about her.

She pulls out a clipboard with a pad of legal-sized paper and hands it to me. "Write down, step by step, everything you did. Which flowers, their amounts, the types of oils you used. Be as exact as possible."

"You mean my perfume? The one you smelled the other day?" I ask incredulously.

"You have more than one?"

"Well, a few," I admit. "But that one's my favorite."

"Do you have a name for it?"

"Texas," I say. The name comes to me in that instant.

"I like it," Mom says. "I can smell the rose in it." She paces a few steps and then turns back. "I can see the bottle now. Clear glass with a yellow-tinted perfume, and a yellow stopper shaped like a rose in full bloom. *Texas.*"

"The rose-shaped stopper has been done too many times, Mom," I say, surprising even myself. "I've always imagined it like this..." I start to sketch on the legal pad. "A full rose head, facing down, in yellow glass, so even when the perfume is almost gone, it still looks pretty." I've drawn it many times before, on drawing pads in my bedroom, on notebooks at school, on napkins in an airplane. "The stopper is all green—it's the stem and ovule with curly sepals." I know it's weird that I know the exact names of the parts of a rose, but with Mom it's better to be scientific. In our family, you know these things. Like other kids know the names of chess pieces or nautical knots. We know flowers.

"That's genius, Lily." Mom paces again. "Fabulous."

What am I doing?

"We'll call it *Texas,* by Lilly Laroche."

What *am* I doing?

Daddy. How does she do it? Pretend like he doesn't exist? I take a deep breath. "No."

Mom's frantically writing her own notes. "We can consider other names." She doesn't look up. "But I do like *Texas*. It's strong, to the point. Sort of masculine. The perfect juxtaposition to the feminine rose."

"Mom…" I close my eyes and gather strength. "It can't be…by…Lily Laroche. My last name's Carter."

"Jasmine uses Laroche as her professional name. It's a trademark. A brand name. Don't be silly." Mom stands up.

I can't let Mom take everything from Dad. Not another daughter. Not his name. Not *me*.

"*Texas,* by Lily Carter, Laroche Cosmetics." It's my final offer. I stare into Mom's eyes, looking for her, the mom in the videos. The mom who loved me.

"Very well then, Lily Carter. You know what you want." Mom actually smiles at me. "*Texas*, by Lily Carter. Laroche Cosmetics." Mom sits back down in her chair. "I always thought Lily Carter was a strong name. Lily Rose Carter. Your dad and I came up with it together. He knew it had to be a flower. That was a given. But he loved the name Lily Rose."

I feel a knot in my throat, imagining Mom and Dad deciding what to name me—together. Both of them agreeing.

"I have some phone calls to make. You stay here in the laboratory and work on your formula." Mom stands up again and heads for the door. "I'm proud of you."

They're the exact same words she said in Paris, only this time they don't sting. Maybe because this time she's actually proud of me for something I'm proud of too.

"Mom... there's one more thing we need to talk about." I dig in my tote for my new *Royale Princesse* marketing plan. Why wait and talk to Mom's producer when I've got the ear of the Empress herself.

Twenty-three

"A woman without perfume is a woman without a future..."

~Coco Chanel

One more day to be a girl. I know sixteen is not actually an adult, but it seems like it. I remember how Jas couldn't wait to turn sixteen, like it was the best thing ever. I'm not so sure. Sometimes I just want to stay a kid, and not have to worry about the things you have to worry about as an adult. Like bikini waxes, for one. Mom says I need one in case I model in a bathing suit. I am *not*. N.O.T. No way. She can forget about it.

Mom, Jas, and I are sitting in a candlelit room in bathrobes, sipping herbal tea, waiting for our next salon treatment. We've already had a facial, our eyebrows done with this piece of thread that the lady twists around each hair and then pulls, and yes, it hurts, and now we'll have our hair and nails done. All for a party that will be held in the dark. Are people really going to notice all of this?

The only thing I'm looking forward to about my birthday is I get to see Dad. As soon as he gets here, I'm going to explain everything and make him take me back home to Texas. I know he wants to keep me away from Dylan, but I'll have no problem convincing Dad it's over. Because it is, and when you tell Dad the truth, he always believes you.

Dad's flying in tomorrow and going straight to the Plaza where my party's being held. I've got it all planned out. I've packed a suitcase, since we'll be staying at the Plaza, too—even though we have Curtis to drive us and live like two seconds away. Then the morning after the party, I'll tell Mom I'm going to Dad's suite to spend some time with him, and I'll never return. After we fly back to Texas, I'll call Mom and tell her I'm done modeling for Laroche cosmetics over the phone. Presto! Problem solved!

Even though yesterday I managed to get Mom to agree to Jas appearing in the next ad, I was still too cowardly to get myself out. That's where Daddy comes in.

Mom's so giddy over my party she doesn't even notice my lack of enthusiasm. We checked in for our triple appointment at Salon di Angelo at nine this morning. I heard Mom tell Curtis we should be done around two in the afternoon. I almost cried. Five hours in a salon? Are we going to be slowly tortured to death?

Jas leans back in her chair and sips her tea. She's

been in a surprisingly good mood the last couple of days, even being nice to me. Although it's not exactly the same as the old days—the Lily-cocoon/Jas-butterfly days. I figure as soon as she finds out she's got her job back, and sees that Chase didn't even come to my party, she'll eventually return to the old Jas.

A stylist enters the room. "What are we doing with Lily's hair today?" she asks Mom, picking up a strand of my hair and examining it. "Keeping the extensions?"

"Can we take them out?" I address my question to Mom. I'd really love to have my own hair back. I can't imagine galloping in the wind on Fire Star with this heavy pile of hair. And just brushing it again, from the scalp down, with no extensions, sounds like heaven. "Please?"

Mom shakes her head. "Your look is a brand now."

"But you said in your book—" I cringe to admit I've even opened it. "That you think heavily applied make-up and hair extensions detract from a woman's natural beauty. It's not the French way, Mom." I may as well use every weapon available—including pulling the French card.

Mom raises her eyebrows and her lips curl ever so slightly. The Hya equivalent of a victory dance. I instantly regret quoting her, but if I lose a few battles in order to win the war, it's worth it.

"Personally, I loathe them," Mom concedes, "but extra-long hair is in vogue this year. We must be pragmatic."

"We could use clip-ins, so she can wear it either way," the stylist offers. She turns to me. "How long is your own hair?"

"About to here. Or maybe longer, now." I point to a spot a few inches below my shoulders. I look at Mom. "I promise I'll wear the extensions when we go out. I really hate these permanent ones. They feel weird." I hold my breath. If she says no, I'll have to go to a salon in Texas and have them removed.

"Fine." Mom exhales. Loudly. "We'll need long human hair clip-ins, then. The very best you have. Exactly her shade."

I want to pump my fist and shout, "Yes!" but I resist the urge. Gloating over my new victories is probably not the best idea. Mom is still Mom. Still the queen. But I've gotten my way with her—two times, in two days. A miracle.

Twenty-four

"The beautiful perfume is that which gets a shock to us." ~Edmond Roudnitska

*I*t might sound crazy, but I love the Plaza. I know it's the polar opposite of simple country décor, with its opulent Louis XV furnishings and gold-gilded everything, but I've come to realize there are two sides of me. I love the open fields, rolling hills, and quiet brooks on the ranch. The dark sky peppered with a million stars. The only sound the chattering of various creatures and the wind. If I could only choose one place to be, I'd choose Texas, hands down. But every time Mom has ever brought me to the Plaza, my heart leaps despite myself. My imagination brings me to a different time, a different world.

I guess it's another thing Mom and I have in common. She's always had an affinity for the Plaza. It was the first hotel in New York that she stayed in when she was a little girl with Meme and Grand-pere, and it captured her heart. Enough for her to leave France and go to Columbia for college, where fate would have her meet a boy from Texas. And when Mom brought Jas and me to New York City for the first time, for a "girl's weekend," when we were only tiny things ourselves, it was to the Plaza. Stepping out of the limo, underneath the flapping entryway flags of the hotel, is a memory permanently emblazoned in my mind.

I can still remember walking down the corridor holding Jas's hand, following Mom, following the bellman. The door to our suite being opened. Jas and I running to the bed and plopping down. Mom chiding us to remove our shoes. The butler handing me a piece of candy and calling me "miss." Jas and I pushing back the curtains and viewing the bright lights of Fifth Avenue for the first time.

For my birthday, Mom has secured the two-bedroom Plaza Suite, not to be confused with the gigantic Royal Plaza Suite, which was deemed unnecessary for only one night after a party, even by Your Royal Highness Herself. Jas asked Mom if Tessa could stay with us too, and she said if it was okay with me, it was okay with her. Well, it's not, but of course I said "sure" while I gritted my teeth, because I have half a mind to join Daddy in his room anyway.

I open the closet where the butler has already unpacked and hung all my clothes, and run my hand along the skirt of my Cinderella costume. It's as beautiful as ever, but without the anticipation of Chase seeing me in it, its magic is gone. Closing the door, I sigh. I turn and climb up on the bed, move the pillows and rest my head on the cream-colored silk headboard. I'm sixteen. Bittersweet sixteen.

Mom and Jas have gone down to a late lunch, but I'm waiting for Daddy. Just knowing he'll be here any minute makes everything better. We can order room service in his suite and catch up—if he gets here soon enough that is, because Gaston will arrive to transform us at exactly four o'clock. I look at the clock next to the bed. Three p.m. Maybe if Gaston does Jas first, there will still be enough time.

The phone rings. I hope it's Dad. Or Chase, hunting me down to change my mind. My heart pounds at the thought of it. He's already been linked with Bibi Johnson again in the tabloids, which I now can't help but scan for his name every chance I get. I remember him telling me on our first date, when we went to see the Statue of Liberty, "Promise me, Lily, that you'll always ask me first, before you ever believe anything you hear about me."

I put the phone to my ear. "Hello?"

"Jas—why aren't you answering your cell phone?"

Tessa. So rude.

"This is Lily."

"Tell Jas I'm coming up."

"She's with Mom in the Rose Club having lunch."

"Fine, I'll find her. My bags are on their way."

I roll my eyes and hang up. I fix the pillows on the bed and make my way to the bathroom. Should I take my make-up off before I see Dad? I wear it most days now, not as much as Mom and Jas do, but at least a little every time we go somewhere. I almost never wore make-up on the ranch, except sometimes for school, and I don't want Dad to think I've changed. I'm still me.

I let the water run from the gold faucet until it feels warm, and grab a fluffy white wash cloth. I hear a knock on the door. Tessa's luggage.

"Come in," I call out.

Another knock. I go to the door.

"Lilykins!"

Daddy stands in the hallway, arms stretched out.

"Dad!" I hold the door open with my foot and hug him, hard. I lay my head against his broad chest, afraid that if I look at him, I might cry. I take a deep breath. "You surprised me!"

"Expecting someone else?" Dad smiles, the corners of his eyes form deep wrinkles, but even so, he still looks young and handsome.

"Just the bellhop!" I take a step back.

"Happy birthday! You look beautiful," Dad says, holding both my hands. "You've been gone just a few weeks and look at you. All grown-up."

He doesn't mention the make-up, but of course he wouldn't. I can't ever remember my Dad embarrassing me. Not ever.

"I'm just down the hall. Get your key and come to my room. I've got something for you."

I grab my key and go with Dad. His room is just as elegant as ours, but a lot smaller. I think about repacking my bags and moving in with him, but he's only got one king bed and one bathroom, and besides, I still have to go through my Gaston treatment. And Mom made it perfectly clear that I'm still on *her* time, as if even inviting Dad to the party was a violation of custody.

I sit at the carved writing desk in Dad's room while he goes into his closet and pulls out a big, beautiful box with a huge bow.

"Aren't you supposed to wait till the party to give me that, Dad?" He's always reminded me of a big kid.

His smile gets even wider. "Okay, if you want to wait…"

I laugh and hold out my hands.

Twenty-five

"Beauty, unaccompanied by virtue, is a flower without perfume." ~French proverb

My transformation is complete; I am now Cinderella, belle of the masquerade ball. Mom is giving me one last inspection in front of the bathroom mirror in our suite, before we head downstairs. She examines me from head to toe, nodding her approval.

There are ornate masks for everyone. Mine is bejeweled and white with a few small feathers on one side. Before I put it on, I take one last look in the mirror. I could probably take a cab to Broadway and walk right on stage in some play.

Even without extensions, my hair is now long and full. Still, Mom had the hairdresser add some extra tonight, for a more dramatic effect. I smooth the almost beehive poof on top my head. Most of my hair is swept back from my face, and all but the bump is in long spiral curls. My make-up has been done to perfection, in all pale beiges and pinks. A delicate tiara sits directly in front of the beehive. I was so relieved when I saw it wasn't a gigantic crown.

"You look stunning," Mom says. "Absolutely gorgeous. I almost hate for you to cover any part of your face." Mom picks the mask up from the vanity and turns it in her hands. "Maybe you shouldn't. Everyone else around you can be disguised. Everyone except for the Princess. The reverse of the historical Cinderella." She puts my mask in her purse. "We'll see."

I shrug. I couldn't care less. Mask or no mask, without Chase it doesn't really matter.

Mom looks at her watch. Dad, Jas, and Tessa went down to the party almost forty-five minutes ago, but Mom is waiting for the perfect timing for my grand entrance.

Finally, Mom says it's time. We walk with Curtis, who Mom made dress like a coachman, to the elevators. Curtis pushes the button, and we wait in silence. Butterflies form in my stomach.

"I've made up my mind," Mom says. "You'll enter wearing the mask, and when you are introduced by the band, you'll remove it."

She's *so* dramatic. Could this get any more embarrassing?

When we get to the doors near the stage, Mom

pulls out my mask and puts it on me carefully, to avoid messing up my hair. "Wait here for exactly five minutes. I need to review the instructions with the MC." She turns to Curtis. "In five minutes, escort her on stage." Mom puts on her own black mask and disappears through the doors. I take a deep breath.

I never realized how long five minutes actually are when you're waiting, standing in heels. Curtis looks down at his watch. "Ready?"

I nod. Ready as I'll ever be to embarrass myself. I might just as well carry a sign in that says, "I AM THE MOST IMPORTANT PERSON IN THIS ROOM!"

I'm glad now that Mom wouldn't let me invite any of my friends from home. "You can have a *Texas* party in the fall," she said. "This is your *New York* party." I guess she forgot I have no friends in New York. Not to worry, Mom provided me with all the fake friends I could never want.

A drum roll announces me and I cringe. The announcer's words jumble in my ears. I'm glad it's dark and noisy. I take a huge breath and use the advice Jas gave me when I was modeling: *make believe.* I make believe that I *am* a princess, a good and noble one, who loves her subjects and is loved by them as well. I walk on stage in a modified Rocco-walk. It's not a runway, so I don't strut, but I don't crawl out like the Hunchback of Notre Dame, either. Not proud, but dignified.

As soon as the crowd has clapped for a few seconds, not the full minute Mom instructed me to wait, I take the mask off and smile at all my guests. My hands shake. I look for Dad. He's close by like he promised, with misty eyes. He looks so proud. Holding out his arm to me, he smiles, and then helps me down.

"My beautiful daughter." He hugs me and twirls me around. "Would you care to dance?"

"Yes, Sire." I laugh and follow Dad's lead. We dance into the crowd. I did it. It's all over now. Sighing with relief, I take in my surroundings. Flickering candles, shimmering crystal, towering topiaries of cream-colored roses. The room is beautiful.

Dad spins me again. I lean into him and finally spit it out. "Can I go home with you tomorrow?"

Dad stops. "Tomorrow?"

Suddenly Mom is there, tapping Dad's shoulder. "Lily *really* must mingle with her guests." She looks at me with steely eyes. "Have you seen Chase?"

Another reason I want to escape with Dad tomorrow. Mom will kill me when she finds out I broke up with Chase. I shake my head and shrug.

Jas and Tessa join us, and as Dad gives Jasmine a squeeze, Tessa gushes over me, suddenly my new best friend. "Happy birthday, Lily!" she singsongs and hugs me, like she didn't just see me an hour ago upstairs. "Come on, let's dance!"

Dad whispers in my ear, "That girl can talk the legs off a chair." He winks at me. "Go ahead, honey. Save me a dance for later."

I give Dad half a smile and reluctantly let Tessa

and Jas lead me out onto the dance floor. It brings back memories of the launch party, just weeks ago. Before I let Chase sweep me off my feet. But I guess even by then it was too late, too late since the moment he first shook my hand and said, *"I'm sorry Jasmine is sick, but lucky me."* His cute, humble smile flashes in my mind and rips at my heart.

The dance floor is crowded with people I don't even know. It's a who's who in the fashion world: designers, models, a few celebrities. Mom really knows how to throw a party. For herself.

More of Jasmine's friends join us, giving me a chance to back away a little from the group and start planning my escape. I've about had it with Tessa. If I hear one more snide remark from her about Chase, I swear I'll smack her. Every time I look at her she's either staring at me or at Jas. I dance in circles, slowly inching away from her.

A guy I've never seen before in a white suit and a fedora turns away from the three girls he's dancing with and shimmies in front of me. He puts one hand behind his head and moves his hips back and forth circling me like some tribal invitation to dance. It's either pretend to dance with him or look rude. I shuffle my feet back and forth as he does all these complex moves in front of me, making me feel like an idiot. His legs slide up and down, nearly to the floor, as his arms move in sharp angles.

One of his dance partners looks annoyed and gives me a once over. She narrows her eyes at me and starts dancing in between us, moving her hips in time with his. It occurs to me that not only are my guests not my friends, but they hate me. I do a little spin and slip further away.

I notice that Jas and Tessa have disappeared, nowhere to be seen. I look around for Dad. He's the only person at my birthday party that I want to be with. Suddenly, strong arms hold me from behind. Familiar arms. My heart races. I turn and face a prince, complete with velvet crown and a white mask.

"Surprise! Happy birthday, Lily!"

Mask or no mask, I'd know those eyes anywhere. I lift the mask.

"Dylan. What are you doing here?"

Dylan picks me up and twirls me around. "Is that any way to greet your boyfriend?" He kisses me straight on the mouth and puts me down. "I've missed you so much."

I gently disengage, not knowing what to do. I planned on telling Dylan the truth about everything, just as soon as I got home, which I was hoping would be tomorrow. "I can't believe you're here!" I shout over the music. "How did you know about this? Who invited you?" *Jas? It has to be. There's no one else.*

"I can't tell you! I'm your surprise birthday present!"

"But my parents, they're both here."

"Thank goodness it's a costume party, then." He pulls the mask back down over his eyes. "Come on, let's dance, pretty lady."

I search the crowd for Jasmine. How could she do this to me? Robotically, I dance with Dylan, my mind racing. If Daddy realizes it's him, I don't know what he'll do. And besides, this will make it that much harder on Dylan when I tell him we're not getting back together. It's cruel. I wanted to let him down easy, but how easy is it to tell a guy who has flown all the way from Houston to New York to attend your birthday party that you were hoping never to see him again?

"So where's Chase Donovan?" Dylan asks looking over my shoulder. "I thought he'd be here."

Gulp. "What do you mean?"

"You think I wasn't watching all summer—you cheating on me with him? We get the news in Texas, too, darlin'. Ah, don't worry about it. Can't blame ya. And your friend told me it was just pretend. For the media." Dylan spins me around and pulls me into his chest. "I need you to do something for me, Lily. Set me up a meeting with him. Get me my big break."

"What friend, Dylan?"

"Huh?"

"What friend told you it was just for the media? Who are you talking about?"

"Aw shucks, I'm not supposed to tell, but I guess you'll find out anyway. Tessa. Your friend Tessa brought me here. Bought my plane ticket and everything. Said you couldn't wait to see me. She even rented me this prince costume."

So it *was* Jas—and her evil sidekick. And to think I gave up Chase for her!

"Dylan, there's been a mistake. We need to talk." I grab his hand and lead him out into the corridor.

"You look so different, Lily. So much prettier." Dylan leans in to kiss me, but I stop him.

"Dylan, listen to me. You are *not* my boyfriend. Remember, my parents said I'm not allowed to see you. I'm sorry you came all this way, but…"

"We didn't *really* break up, Lily. I told you I'd wait for you."

"I didn't tell you the same. I'm sorry, Dylan. It's not true what Tessa said about Chase. It wasn't just for the press…"

Dylan grabs my arm and squeezes hard. "Does this mean you're not going to introduce me? I need that break."

"What you need is to get out of here before my Dad sees you." I pull my arm away.

"You think you can just end it with me that easily? Put airs on like some princess and just kick me to the curb?" He grabs my arm again. "I'm not good enough for you anymore. Is that it?"

I should be mad at him for hurting my arm, but his words hurt me even more. Do I think I'm too good for him? The truth is, I do, but it isn't because he's not rich or famous. That's the only part I *like* about him. "Dylan, I'm sorry. I'm not too good for you. You were the first boy who ever asked me out. I wanted to give it a try…" I close my eyes and breathe deep. "I've changed."

"You've got that right. Look at you, all that make-up and hair. You're a fake."

"I've changed on the *inside*, Dylan. I can take all this make-up off and go back to Texas tomorrow, but I still won't be the same girl you knew."

"Then let me *get* to know you…" Dylan cups my chin with his hand and leans in like he's going to kiss me.

"Dylan, stop. I didn't know myself before…" I put my hand over his and gently bring it down. "But I know *you*, and this won't work. Not for either of us."

Click. Click, click, click. A camera flashes around us.

"Dylan. Dylan Richards, right?" A single photographer has gotten past security.

Dylan smiles and poses for the camera, putting his arm around my back. "That's me."

Click. Click.

"Stop!" I yell. All I can think of is Chase. Chase reading the headlines. Chase believing that Dylan is "the someone" I said I couldn't hurt by being with him. I stand up and put my hand in front of the camera. "Please stop!"

I run down the corridor toward the elevators. Looking back, I see Dylan posing for more pictures and talking to the photographer. I push the button and wait. The door opens and I run straight into Jas and Tessa. "Ooooooh! I hate you!" I scream, backing away and running further down the hall. I take the stairs.

I race up two flights and then go back into a

hallway to find the elevators again. Ten more flights on the stairs when my feet are already killing me? I don't think so. I push the elevator button and pull off my shoes. The doors open. Jas and Tessa again. I turn and run.

"Lily, wait!" Jas gets out of the elevator and runs after me with Tessa right behind her.

I reach the stairwell and stop, then turn to face them. "How could you, Jas? Why hurt so many people?"

"What are you talking about?"

"My 'surprise' Jas. Sending Dylan here. It was cruel. To him. To me." I choke on my words. "To Chase."

"I did *not* bring Dylan here. I would *never* do that."

We turn and look at Tessa. She throws both hands in the air. "Hey—it was his idea. Sometimes when he'd call Jas's cell phone looking for you, I'd answer and give him a hard time." She shrugs her shoulders. "Jas wouldn't give him the time of day."

"I told you he was a jerk, Tessa. How could you do this?" Jas crumples to the floor and leans against the wall, her green ball gown pooling around her like a lily pad.

"The guy said he needed a break. He's desperate to meet Chase Donovan." Tessa takes a step toward Jas. "And I thought it would be the perfect revenge after what Lily did to you. How long have you been in love with Chase Donovan? Your whole life revolved around meeting him and doing that ad campaign. And she just stole the whole thing away from you. The fame, the money, the guy."

I stand face to face with Tessa. "Fine. I deserve to be punished." My voice rises. "But did it ever occur to you that it's wrong to use some innocent guy for revenge?"

"Innocent? Did you see him back there? He didn't come here for *you*. He came here to have his fifteen minutes of fame. Give me a break." Tessa slides down the wall and sits on the floor across from Jas. She looks at me. "I thought it would be funny. I thought Chase would be here, and then when he saw Dylan, he'd break up with you. Look on the bright side. At least Chase isn't here yet. Have your mother's bozos kick Dylan out. Blame it on me."

Jas glares at Tessa. "You're an idiot! The whole world will know he was here. That paparazzi guy probably already downloaded the pictures to the internet. I could kill you!"

Tessa tosses her head and gestures toward me. "What about her? *She* took the love of your life!"

I slump down next to Jas and pull off my tiara. "I never meant to...to...take...him...or your job. I'm so sorry." I lean my head against the wall and look up at the ceiling. "Chase isn't coming. I broke up with him, Jas, that last night in Paris. And I'm not doing any more perfume ads."

"You broke up with him? You're both idiots! I don't even like Chase anymore. Jacques' flight landed almost an hour ago. He'll be here any minute."

Tessa looks at Jas with disgust. "What happened to your 'master plan' to snag the world's hottest pop star?"

"You mean the world's biggest nerd?" Jas turns to me. "When I saw that weird Shakespeare letter he wrote you, I knew you two were meant for each other. He's totally not my type."

I broke up with Chase for nothing? I throw my tiara at Tessa. "Here. I now crown you the wicked witch of the Upper West Side." I get up off the floor and start down the hall.

"Lily—wait." Jas gets up, too. "I wish you wouldn't have, but thanks for breaking up with Chase for me." Jas takes her cell phone out of her glittery clutch and holds it out to me. "I still have his number. Call him. Explain everything. If you don't, I will."

"It's too late, Jas."

"It's never too late."

I take a deep breath. "Let's just go back to the party. There's been enough drama for one night already. For Dad, I'll stay at the party until they cut the cake."

Jas puts her arm around me. "That's my little sister. Take the bull by the horns."

"What about Dylan?" Tessa looks at us sheepishly.

"I'll convince Dad that he's no threat. The damage is already done. Let him stay." I point to Tessa. "But *you* entertain him."

"Can I still crash in your room tonight?" Tessa

looks hopeful.

Jas narrows her eyes at Tessa and lunges for her. "Are you kidding me? Take your flying monkeys and get out of here."

I grab Jas's arm. "Let her stay a little longer. So she can take care of Dylan."

Jas shakes her head and puts her arm around me. "You're the most kind-hearted person I know. Wimp!" She turns and grabs the tiara out of Tessa's hand and places it on my head. "Put this back on. It's your birthday."

"No." I take the tiara off. "I like it better in the shadows. When *you* shine. I don't want to be in the spotlight anymore, Jas. That's where you belong."

"Are you forgetting one of Hya's greatest rules? 'Let yourself shine!' You don't make anyone else's light brighter by hiding your own."

I look down at the crown, not sure what to do.

"Put the tiara on, Lily," Jas whispers. "There's room for more than one princess in the world."

Twenty-six

"The friendship without confidence, it is a flower without perfume." ~Laure Conan

The three of us walk to the elevators and stop in front of an ornate Louis XV mirror. I fix the tiara on my head and look at my reflection. "There's just one thing missing," I say. "I need to stop in the room before we go back to the party."

"You look great," Jas says. "What do you need? I've got lip gloss in my purse."

"You'll see."

We go to the room, and I take the big, beautifully-wrapped gift box that Daddy gave me this afternoon out of the closet. I open the lid and pull them out. The most gorgeous pair of sparkling white cowboy boots you've ever seen. I slip off my Cinderella shoes and pull on my brand-new boots.

Lifting my dress, I turn from side to side. "How do they look?"

"Ridiculous," Tessa says.

"Perfect," Jas says giving me a big hug. "There's no rule against being a princess *and* a cowgirl."

We both laugh.

"Come on. Let's go party!" I link arms with Jas. I've got my sister—and my cowgirl—back. *And* I can still be a princess. I feel a pang in my heart for Chase, but I guess you can't have your cake and eat it, too.

I hang on to one hope. Chase did say he doesn't read the tabloids. Doesn't even *look* at them. Doesn't *believe* them. I cross my fingers and hope that he'll never see the picture of Dylan and me together.

As soon as we exit the elevators we're practically accosted by Curtis. "Found them," he says into his mouth piece. "We'll be right there." He turns to us. "Your mother's been looking everywhere for you. There's a commotion with some party crasher."

My heart sinks. Dad's an easygoing guy—but when it comes to Dylan...

"We know," Jas says. "Dylan Richards is here. What did you do with him?"

Curtis points down the corridor. "He's being interrogated. By your mother."

I'm shaking in my cowboy boots. One look at

Tessa and it's clear she's so scared she might faint. Her eyes are bulging out and her lips are trembling. Jas, on the other hand, is perfectly calm. She grabs my hand and walks straight into the line of fire.

Dylan is slouched on an upholstered divan surrounded by two security guards. Mom and Dad are standing in front of him. I just hope we aren't too late and Mom hasn't called 911 or something worse.

Mom's head spins the moment she sees me. "What's the meaning of this, Lily? What about Chase? This could ruin the perfume campaign!"

"This isn't about perfume, Hya," Dad interrupts. "This is about trust." He looks at me. "I thought we made it clear you weren't supposed to see this guy anymore."

"I didn't, Dad. I mean, I haven't even talked to him all summer. Until tonight."

"It's my fault." Jas gets between me and them. She motions for Tessa to leave. Out of the corner of my eye, I see Tessa slowly backing up toward the double doors that lead into the party. She better move fast.

"He found out about the party from one of my friends," Jas says. "She invited him. Lily knew nothing about it."

"It's true, Mr. Carter," Dylan says. "I saw a number from New York on my caller ID one night, the same day Lily started modeling. When I called it back, no one ever answered, until one day I got this chick named Tessa."

Mom rolls her eyes. "Heavens!" She looks around

for Tessa who, luckily for her, has escaped. "So you come to this party dressed as a prince?"

"That was part of the surprise. Tessa said I was supposed to."

"*Chase* is her prince!" Mom's voice rises. She turns to Dad. "Do something!" Then to Curtis. "There were pictures taken!"

Dad and Curtis look at her, and then each other, like they have no idea what to do.

"Must I do everything?" Mom shrieks. "Dylan, where did that photographer go? Do you remember his name?"

"They kicked him out." Dylan tosses his head toward the security guards. "But he gave me his phone number." Dylan reluctantly hands Mom a crumpled-up business card and then hangs his head. "He wants to do a story on me."

Mom grabs the card. "We have to do something before Chase gets here. Curtis! Your phone!"

I finally find my voice. "Mom. Look at me. Chase isn't—"

"Going to care," I hear Chase's voice say behind me.

Twenty-seven

"To create new arrangements, new olfactory forms, it is enough that you think in odors, like the painter in colors, and the musician in sounds..." ~Edmond Roudnitska

I turn, holding my breath. My prince has come, but why? For the ad campaign? For his mom? My mom? *Me?*

"Who is this dude?" Dylan snarls.

I have to laugh. Chase is standing in front of me dressed from head to toe as a cowboy, not a prince. Mom's jaw drops.

"You must be Dillard." Chase shakes Dylan's hand. "Chase Donovan. Nice to meet you." He turns to me. "Happy birthday, Lily."

Mom looks like she might faint.

"Why are you here?" It's probably not the most

romantic thing to say when a cowboy comes to rescue you, or the best response to "happy birthday," but I need to be sure. For all I know, there could have been a rider on Mom's contract: must attend all publicity events. And that's exactly what my birthday party is. Publicity.

"Lily." Moms finds her voice quickly. "Where are your manners?"

"Thanks," I say to Chase. "For coming."

Dylan puts his arm around my shoulders. "The name's Dylan. Dylan Richards. Lily's *real* boyfriend."

I push his arm down. "Dylan, we broke up."

"You didn't mean it, Lily. You were probably just startled to see me here." Dylan puts his arm around me again. I shrug him off, but it's too late.

Chase looks at me, "When did you guys break up?"

"Uh…" My mind races.

"About an hour ago," Dylan says. "But hey listen, no hard feelings." He pats Chase on the back. "I'm a musician, too." He pulls out a CD.

No! He didn't! I wish I could disappear!

"Dylan, put that away," I hiss.

"No hard feelings about what?" Chase asks Dylan, completely ignoring me.

"About you dating my girl all summer. I know… she explained it to me. Publicity for the perfume. It wasn't real." Dylan tries to put his arm around me again. Is he a Neanderthal? I elbow him.

"Well if you'll excuse me, I'm here to do a *job*."

Chase shakes Dylan's hand again and nods to me. "Lily," he says coolly, and walks through the double doors into the party.

For the first time ever, I wish Hya would do something. She's just standing there looking like the Cheshire cat, like she's just eaten a bird or something, her mouth twisted. I've heard her say before that sometimes a controversy is the best publicity of all. Please tell me she hasn't changed her mind and is embracing this change of events.

"Everyone inside," Mom orders. "Take him in, too," she says to the security guards, pointing at Dylan. "Where I can keep my eye on him."

We enter the ballroom and stop just inside the doors. I watch numbly as Chase walks to the stage and climbs the stairs. He takes the microphone. "Let's hear it for the birthday girl!" His voice cracks and I notice he has pushed his cowboy hat further down on his forehead, so that it shadows his eyes. I choke back tears.

Applause erupts. Mom forces me closer to the stage. I stand mesmerized as Chase picks up his guitar and sits down on a stool, his eyes still veiled by his cowboy hat. He strums the guitar for what seems like forever, and then I hear his voice. His clear, beautiful voice. He's singing a new song. A song I've never heard before. A country song. A song for me?

Beautiful girl,

Let yourself shine,

Your heart is like gold,

Please let it be mine,

When the sun sets on the desert rose,

And its petals close till morning light,

I think of you...

When stars appear in the Texas sky,

Yet fade away at the first ray of dawn,

I think of you...

When storms gather,

And the sun hides behind the clouds,

I think of you...

Afraid to shine,

Beautiful girl,

Afraid to shine,

Beautiful Girl,

Let yourself shine,

Your heart is like gold,

Please let it be mine...

When Chase is finished, he simply says, "Happy birthday, Lily," walks off the stage, and disappears through the doors. I can't breathe. I will never, ever, breathe again.

I stand frozen in time. My eyes closed.

"Find him, Lily." Jas shakes me. "Don't be an idiot. Go!" She pushes me.

Dylan starts to open his mouth.

"Don't even try," Jas says to him.

Mom looks sternly at Dylan. "It's time for you to leave." She turns to Curtis, about to give orders, but I stop her.

"I got this," I say. I turn to Dylan. "I'm sorry how this all happened. Really, I am. But it's over." I take a deep breath. "Goodbye, Dylan. Tessa will take you to the airport now."

I turn and leave, not looking behind, and walk in the direction I saw Chase go. I put my shoulders back, stand up straight, and do my new walk, definitely toned down from Rocco's version, but not my coward's walk from before. I'm going after what I want.

Twenty-eight

"Forgiveness is the fragrance that the violet sheds on the heel that has crushed it." ~Mark Twain

"Chase, wait!" I see him in the hallway with his bodyguards, walking toward the elevators. He stops and turns when he hears me. As I get closer, he hands his hat to one of his bodyguards and takes one step toward me.

I stop a few feet away and take a deep breath. "Don't leave."

He searches my eyes and we stand motionless. The words got stuck in my throat. How can I ever explain?

As if he doesn't need me to, Chase suddenly opens his arms to me. I go the rest of the way and throw my arms around him.

"What about Dillard?" It's nearly a whisper.

I look up at him and try to explain. "It wasn't exactly true what he said, it wasn't like that. Ever since I met you... no, even before. You see, my parents…"

Chase laughs. "It's okay, Lily. Is your heart mine?"

"Yes. It always was. Tessa brought him here. Not me. I didn't break up with you because of him, or him because of you." I close my eyes. "It's complicated."

"Then why don't you tell me the whole story tomorrow? I'm not going anywhere." He lifts my chin. "Tonight, we'll celebrate your birthday."

"Perfect." I look into his eyes and see everything I need to know. "Thank you for the song, Cowboy."

"You're welcome, Princess."

I laugh and pull my gown high enough to reveal my cowboy boots.

Chase laughs, too, picks me up, and spins me around. "Would you like to dance?" he whispers in my hair. "Cowgirl Princess."

Twenty-nine

"Sometimes one finds an old bottle which remembers from where all spouts out lives a heart which returns." ~Baudelaire

"May I cut in?" Dad taps Chase on the shoulder and holds his arms out to me. "Ready for that dance you promised?"

"Sir…" Chase tips his hat to Dad and lets me go.

Dad rustles me like a calf into the middle of the crowded dance floor. We spin and twirl and then settle into an easy rhythm.

"Sorry about Dylan, Dad."

He laughs. "I always knew that boy was all hat and no horse. How's this other young man treating you?"

I try to think of the best way to put it. "Like you, Dad."

Dad grins. "That's my girl." He puts a little more

distance between us, so he can see my face. "What were you saying earlier about coming home with me? I thought you were kind of enjoying your new job."

I swallow hard. I've worried all summer long what Dad thought of me—if it hurt him to see me work for Mom. I have to be honest with Dad, tell him the truth. I owe him that. "I did like some of it, I mean, I do. But what I really like is making perfume. Not modeling."

Dad's quiet for a moment. He studies my face. "Would you like to live here with Mom in New York for awhile, and make perfume?"

"No! I would never live with Mom. I can make all the perfume I want back home. With you." I hold him tight.

"Sweetheart, look at me." Dad separates us again, holding both my shoulders. "It's okay to love your mom. Forgive her, Lily. I have."

"How, Dad? How do you forgive—that?" A familiar tight feeling squeezes my chest.

"Do you forgive *me*?"

"For what? You're not the one who left. You're not the one who threw our family out like last season's fashion fad."

Dad is quiet. He has to know I'm right. What can he say?

"We all make mistakes, Lily. We all have dreams. Some of us are just stronger, or maybe…weaker…than others." Dad sighs. "I don't know if I'm making any sense. I don't mean it was right what happened, how it happened. It wasn't. But I know she loves you."

I'm sure Mom loves me in her own way. I didn't need Dad to tell me, or even Mom. And not because she signs everything to me, "All my love," because saying it, or writing it, is so different from showing it by what you *do*. But I guess that's what Dad means by some of us are weaker. I don't know if Dad thinks Mom's the strong one, and he's been weak, but if that's what he means, he's wrong. I will always believe it takes more strength to hold on, than to let go.

"I love you, Dad." I lay my head against the starchy fabric of his suit. "You're the best dad in the whole state of Texas."

"Only Texas?" Dad grins.

"Does anywhere else count?"

Thirty

"The gods create the odors, the men manufacture the perfumes." ~Jean Giono

"Everyone, please be seated." Mom stands at the front of the viewing room, eyes surveying her loyal—and not so loyal—subjects. She nods to the producer when it appears that everything is in order, and then sits down next to Jas and me.

Her ad team has put together the main part of the next commercial for the *Royale Princesse* perfume campaign, phase two, with my idea, and Mom agreed to let it be a surprise for Jas. I can't wait for her to see it. The lights go down and the ad comes on the screen. I hold my breath.

The producer has converted the video to black

and white, and it moves in short clips. Jas and I as young girls, in white linen dresses, running up the stairs of a French castle, playing dress up, riding ponies. The final clip shows Jas as an adorable little girl, sitting in a puffy wingchair wearing a tiara, dressed as a princess, and making a sweet face for the camera. *Royale Princesse* flashes across the screen, and then the gorgeous bottle of perfume. *Never forget your inner princess...* the commercial says.

The director interrupts the silence. "We'll add some footage of Jasmine and Lily, as the beautiful young women they are today, at the end. Something fun, like the two of them having lunch at an outdoor café, laughing over a secret." He turns up the lights. "I think it's brilliant. Remind all women, the young and the more mature, to always remain a princess at heart."

I look over at Jas. She's dabbing at her eyes to stop the tears. "It's beautiful. It's perfect. But what about Chase? I thought he was the main attraction."

"Sales of *Royale* are strong, and this ad will reach an even larger audience." Mom rises to her feet. "Besides, we'll be launching a new perfume next season, *Texas,* and maybe we can talk Lily into doing one more campaign—with Chase."

"I'll consider it." I sit up tall in my seat. "But just one." I smile at Jas. "I think I'll stick to making perfume from now on."

Thirty-one

"Happiness is the perfume of the heart, the harmony of the heart which sings." ~Romain Rolland

$\mathcal{I}$'m galloping Fire Star across the prairie at full speed. Back in my beloved Texas. My long hair, which is all mine, and Fire Star's mane, blow in the wind. It's April, and wild flowers have sprung up everywhere: blue bonnets, verbena, yellow Texas daisies, foxglove. We reach the top of a grassy hill overlooking a small creek. I dismount and let Fire Star loose, knowing she'd never wander far, and sit on a rock.

My favorite place on earth.

I spend more time in New York now than I ever have, visiting Mom and Jas even when I don't have to. But there's no place like home. No place like Texas.

Taking a deep breath, I say a quick prayer of gratitude. This is where I belong. Almost every day after school and every weekend morning, I ride to this very spot. Who could be luckier?

Jas comes more often to visit me and Dad since the events of last summer, so I guess some good things came out of my whirlwind modeling stint. I'm closer to Jas, can almost tolerate Mom on a good day, and I know, just a little better, who I am.

And there's another good thing that came out of last summer...

Chase rides up the hill toward me on a dark bay horse. When he reaches me, he dismounts and lets his horse join Fire Star, who's now eating grass only a few yards away. He walks toward me, and I can tell he's fighting the urge to laugh out loud.

"Cut!" the director shouts. "I liked the way we did it the first time better, with the two of them riding up on only one horse. Lily and Chase together."

So do I.

Acknowledgements

I'm so grateful to my mother, grandmothers, and aunts, who always taught me the best rules to live by. Cyndie Gloe, the queen of good sisters. Kerry O' Malley Cerra, who hauled me to my first writing group, encouraged me to join the Society of Children's Book Writers and Illustrators, and has done so much for me there isn't enough space to write it all down. The indispensible Michelle Delisle, who has shared with me her time and knowledge beyond measure. Dorian Cirrone, royal grammar expert, gifted editor, and generous mentor. Kelly Pulido, talented photographer and artist. Cheryl Bivins, who reads, rereads, and reads again. Jill MacKenzie, my kindred spirit writing pal. Members of my loyal writing group, past and present, Meredith McCardle, Nicole Cabrera, Jodi Wayne Sandel, and Susan Safra. My fabulous beta-readers, Amy Kuebler, Neia Gwaltney, April Petito, and Laurie Kelliher. My husband and son, for their infinite love and patience. My "extra" daughters, Kylie, Nanci, Mary, Emily, Kayla, Ashley, Sabrina and Stefanie. This book was inspired by all of you!

And especially, my very first reader, my daughter Gaby, who reads every word, page by page, whenever I ask.

About the Author

Kristina Miranda lives in South Florida with her knight in shining armor, a prince and a princess, and three royal canines. You can visit her online at www.KristinaMiranda.com

Made in the USA
San Bernardino, CA
10 April 2017